The Oxley Crossing Romances

Australian Rural Romance

Saving
Jonathon Armitage

Lena West

Gymea Publishing

Published by Gymea Publishing

Copyright © 2017 Lena West and Gymea Publishing.

https://www.facebook.com/LenaWestAuthor/

www.lenawestauthor.com

ISBN-13: 978-0-6482110-2-0

Disclaimer

This story is a work of fiction.

Names, characters, places and incidents are the product of the author's imagination and are used fictitiously. Any resemblance to events, locales or actual persons, living or dead, is entirely coincidental.

Some actual locations may be referenced in passing.

Table of Contents

SAVING JONATHON ARMITAGE

Dedication

To my wonderful mother.

SAVING JONATHON ARMITAGE

1

"Oh, very nice." Megan Patterson shifted for a clearer view of the service station apron.

"What? What's very nice? C'mon Megs, give."

"Sorry Geni. Momentarily distracted. I was admiring a very nice, late model Harley that pulled in for fuel just now. Black with chrome trim. Never mind, go on with what you were saying." Megan shifted the phone to her other ear, eyes still glued to the motorbike that had caught her eye.

"Never mind the Harley, Megs. What's the Harley's rider like? He's got to be more interesting than my rant about my soon-to-be ex. Is he a spunk, or a hog?"

"A spunk, far as I can see." Megan laughed as she always did when Geni voiced her nonsensical interest in some man. Any man.

"Tell me more. You know Megs, this is half your trouble, you know," Geni Sullivan's voice took on a censorious tone. "If, just occasionally, you noticed the man rather than the machine, you might have landed yourself one by now and be happy as a pig in mud with half a dozen kids and an adoring husband. So, let's start practising. Right now. Go on, take a good look at this bloke on the Harley and tell me what you see."

Megan laughed again, then decided to play along with her friend. After all, Geni still lived in Sydney. Too far away to push her into any more blind dates or difficult foursomes in her crusade to 'find Megan a man'.

In Megan's opinion, Geni was a prime example of the problems you incurred if you chose badly, ending up with someone who fell way short of being Mr Absolutely Perfect. With the example of her parents' happy, loving marriage as her benchmark, she'd long ago decided she'd rather wait till she was sure.

Only she hadn't really expected the wait to be so long. Just lately she'd seriously begun to question whether she'd set her expectations unreasonably high. Thinking that maybe she ought to settle for Mr Pretty Good. Shaking herself out of her moment of introspection she applied herself to Geni's exercise.

"Let's see." The subject of the exercise was swinging a long, well-proportioned leg over the bike propped onto its stand beside the pump. Megan's eyes opened a little wider, studying the man now with a coolly critical, though admiring eye. And she found plenty to admire. "Tall, black leathers, snug fitting," she began reciting, then continued. "Oh good, no club insignia. Lean, slim-hipped. A derrière my palms itch to fondle." She grinned, knowing Geni would appreciate the titillating extra.

"Keep going, you're doing fine."

"Don't be so impatient Geni. Ah, the helmet's off." The man shook out a sweat-damp, dark wavy mane that brushed his shoulders, so Megan added that to her description. "Can't see his face yet. Oh, he's taking off his jacket, Geni. White T-shirt, sweat stained. Must be hot under the helmet and full leathers, even though the weather's still a bit cool. Broad shoulders, good muscle definition. Lean, work-hardened muscles, you know, not pumped up from working out in the gym."

Megan ran out of steam at that point. Until the man turned his face towards her, she had nothing to add. Nothing she cared to tell Geni, anyway.

No way was she going to tell her friend about the butterflies stirring in her stomach. No way. If she did, she'd never hear the end of it. Just the same, she let her eyes rove over the attractive masculine figure outside the office window, this time solely for her own pleasure.

Hanging up the nozzle, the rider turned to walk into the office; and the butterflies fluttered their wings.

"Early thirties I'd guess. Good-looking," she added to the tally then finished up in a hurry. "Gotta go Geni. He's coming in. Bye." Snapping the phone off before her friend had time to say another word, she slipped it into the pocket of her tattered gardening jeans.

Lively blue eyes tracked the Harley's rider through the door. A smile still lingering on her face from the nonsense with Geni, Megan surreptitiously studied the high cheeked-boned, tanned face; mouth drying and smile fading as the butterflies beat their wings more energetically.

3

Alarmed at her unexpected physical reaction, Megan gulped, struggling to quell a sudden attack of nerves when, totally shocked, she identified her unfamiliar feelings as pure lust.

Ignoring her, he crossed straight to the fridge, helping himself to a carton of chocolate milk; her favourite too. Was that a good sign or not? *'Sign of what, for God's sake?'* She asked herself. Half-heartedly, she tried to divert her thoughts only to fail in the next instant.

Impatiently tearing the carton open he gulped the milk down straight from the carton. A tendril of sensual delight curled upward through Megan's body and her fingers longed to reach out and sweep those untidy locks back from the wide forehead as her eyes followed the swallowing movement of the Adam's apple bobbing in his throat.

Embarrassed by her unwonted voyeurism, Megan strove to banish her alarming reactions to this chance-encountered stranger. *'It's Geni's fault,'* she grumbled to herself, *'making me way too aware of his attractions.'* It wasn't her normal practice to ogle strangers as if she'd never seen a good-looking man before.

'Still,' an inner voice that sounded a lot like Geni argued, *'it's a free world. A girl can always look, can't she?'* Surely there was no harm in that. Even so, Megan had the uncomfortable presentiment she was straying onto dangerous ground, and hurriedly dropped her eyes. Just in time.

The rider turned face-on, for the first time giving Megan an unobstructed view of shuttered, steely grey eyes and a tight, keep-your-distance expression. She shivered, the butterflies folding their wings abruptly when she encountered chilly indifference in the look turned on her by the man she'd been guiltily fantasising over.

Megan had little personal vanity, her self-image being of wholesome ordinariness instead of the alluring siren she'd once dreamed of becoming. During her early years she had been consistently passed over as girlfriend material by the male of the species. As a child she had been a tomboy, a welcome extra to make up the cricket or football team; later a knowledgeable admirer of their cars, the confidante to whom they poured out their troubles.

Always their buddy, but never any man's love.

Apparently, whatever it was that attracted men in *that* way was in short supply in herself; a fact she'd long been reconciled to. Confidant of one day finding her own particular mate, and unwilling to settle for second best, Megan had refused to let it trouble her, enjoying herself without becoming too closely involved with the men she'd met in the city. Attractive, entertaining men some of them, but none who affected her deeply.

No man had ever touched her guarded heart.

Instinct warned her that this man was intangibly different.

This man aroused unfamiliar longings within her. Disturbing longings to be more than she knew herself to be. More beautiful. More vivacious. *'More sexy,'* whispered that treacherous inner voice. More everything.

With a disparaging downwards glance at her appalling gardening clothes a sigh issued silently through lips that momentarily assumed an unaccustomed droop.

Stranger though he was, this man's coldness for some inexplicable reason, had the power to hurt her.

'*The sooner he's on his bike and out of here again, the better,*' she thought crossly, mentally shaking off her pain as she accepted his money.

Defiantly meeting his eyes with a stare aloof enough to match his own, Megan accidentally brushed his fingers as she handed over his change. A tiny, but very definite, electric charge almost had her dropping the coins. Nothing like *that* had ever happened to her before! Startled by the unexpected tingle, she stifled a gasp and had to work at retaining her equilibrium.

Instead of taking himself off immediately, the oh-so-annoying man hovered in front of Megan, as if trying to make up his mind about something.

"Anything else I can help you with?" she asked, professionally polite, still matching him cool stare for cool stare while willing him on his way.

Abruptly making his mind up, he nodded towards the sign in the window.

**MECHANIC WANTED
APPLY WITHIN**

"That job. Is it still available?" His low baritone, heard for the first time, matched his cold expression.

Megan's heart sank.

The Lord knew, she desperately needed to find a mechanic, and soon, or her father's garage would be forced to close. His customers were loyal, but they couldn't be expected to wait forever. Work was piling up and soon his customers would be turning elsewhere. Only couldn't her first applicant, make that only applicant, have been someone who didn't unsettle her as this man did?

"Yes, the job's still available," she answered reluctantly. "Are you applying for it?" Megan had to work even harder now to keep her own voice and eyes cool and non-committal.

He nodded, eyes sliding past Megan to look out the window. Dismissing her. As if making up his mind, he swung to face her again, his gaze now sharply focused.

"Who do I talk to?"

So he was serious. Megan bit her lip, thinking quickly. Her need for a mechanic outweighed her personal wariness; and, she reminded herself, beggars couldn't afford to be choosers. Since she'd received no other expressions of interest, she ought to be jumping for joy instead of wanting to brush him off.

"You talk to me," she stated crisply, decision made. "I take it you have all the necessary paperwork. Trade qualifications, references, etcetera?" All business now, Megan looked him in the eye, informing him in no uncertain manner that she was in charge.

"In my saddlebags." He hesitated, and Megan cut in, eager now not to let opportunity slip through her fingers.

"Go and get them then, why don't you. You're here anyway and since it's a slow morning I can fit in an interview right away, if you like."

Shrugging, he went outside and moved his bike away from the pumps before digging in the saddlebag for his document folder.

God knew, he needed a job, but did it have to be out here in the middle of nowhere? He'd seen an ad in the 'Tamworth Times' at breakfast, and on impulse had decided to try for it. Only Oxley Crossing was way out in the sticks, and he was a city boy. What the bloody hell was he doing out here?

He'd almost turned back, after miles of nothing but bush, dusty sheep and widely scattered farmhouses; except that his stubborn streak had kicked in, insisting he follow through on what he'd started. *'Looks like I'm about to rejoin the ranks of the employed,'* he thought sourly. He wouldn't be staying long though, just until he had a few dollars in his kitty again; then they wouldn't see him for dust. The few shops he'd noticed on his slow burbling progression down the main street had represented all the basic necessities, and a handful of extras, but absolutely nothing in the way of entertainment except for the pub. Not his kind of town, that's for sure.

Offering coffee, or another cold drink if he preferred, Megan led the way to one of the tables across the room from the cash register. Immediately setting a friendly, impersonal tone for the interview, she introduced herself, extending her hand to him as she did so.

"Megan Patterson. My father owns this service station and garage. Usually he runs it himself, but he's laid up for a month or two and we need a stand-in mechanic."

There it was again! That electric tingle when their hands touched. Frowning briefly, he glanced at his hand, then shook it slightly and wiped it across his shirt as he took his seat.

So, he felt it too. Megan wondered fleetingly what caused it. *'Probably just static electricity,'* she answered herself, then concentrated her mind on the interview.

"Jon Armitage," the biker offered in response to Megan's introduction. "So you're only looking for someone on a temporary basis. How long for?"

"It depends on the doctors, really, but I expect it will be a minimum of two to three months." *'Please don't let him be put off by the lack of permanency,'* Megan prayed silently. The ads in the papers had been running for over a week already, producing no more interest than the sign in the window. Until today. Few people were interested in working in a little country place like Oxley Crossing; even fewer when the job was temporary.

"Two or three months should be okay," Jon agreed after taking a moment to consider." I take it it's a one-man operation? No apprentices or assistants?"

"That's right. Just Dad, since he took over from my grandfather twenty years ago. You wouldn't have to worry about the pumps at all, we have other people to handle that; just the mechanical side. If you're interested, let me see your papers. If they're satisfactory, we can talk business."

As Megan browsed carefully through his file, stopping to clarify a point here and there, Jonathon Armitage went up a notch or two in her estimation.

It required an effort not to let him see how impressed she was.

"Good qualifications," Megan conceded coolly. "The references look good too, but you do realise I'll have to verify them, don't you?" she challenged, looking him straight in the eye.

"Of course. No problem." He shrugged, totally unconcerned.

'He's very confident they'll check out well,' Megan observed. She had begun to see Jonathon Armitage in a new light; as a potential asset for the business. And for herself? Shocked, she shied away from answering that question, wondering where it had sprung from. *'Damn Genie and her nonsense.'*

"How long do you expect that to take you?"

Jonathon Armitage's question pulling her attention back from disturbing personal questions to the business at hand, Megan calculated swiftly.

"If I can reach your referees immediately, no more than an hour or so. I'll get on the phone right away. In the meantime, why don't you take a look around the town. Have some lunch. By then I should be able to give you an answer."

Megan gave him a cool, professional smile and waved him towards the door; this time carefully avoiding his hand. Most likely it was only static electricity she felt when they touched; but then again, maybe it wasn't.

Nodding his agreement, Jon walked off, passing an older man just entering; one who wore a petroleum company logo on his uniform jacket. Lean and balding with a droopy moustache, he frowned forbiddingly at the darkly handsome young man in black leathers and T-shirt.

"Who was that young fella Meggie? It's not like you to sit around with strangers who blow into town." Half inquisitive and half protective, he let his concern for Megan show, defusing her flash of irritation at his implied criticism. Jack O'Hara had been best man at her parents' wedding; had known her all her life, always treating her like one of his own daughters. Knowing his nosiness was kindly meant, Megan welcomed him with a warm smile.

"That young fella, Jack," she informed him smugly, "is our new mechanic. As long as his references are as good as they look. His trade qualifications are excellent. Now that you're back, I'll head over to my own office. Send him across when he comes back, will you please, Jack?"

SAVING JONATHON ARMITAGE

2

Giving Jack another quick, confident smile, Megan walked next door, to the old bank building. Freshly painted, it was almost ready to reopen for business.

When the building, with its business premises at the front and spacious two storied living quarters at the back, had come on the market she'd snapped it up, committing herself and her hard-won nest egg to a future in Oxley Crossing.

Returning to live in The Crossing, a fully-fledged, experienced accountant, Megan had soon perceived an opening for her professional services.

Although it had never been her intention to stay, she'd reassessed her priorities, changed her career direction and begun building up a local clientele. The old bank building provided both abundant office space and living quarters.

Next door to her parents' home, where she had grown up in the flat above the service station, yet maintaining her independence, she had been on hand throughout the last months of her mother's losing battle with breast cancer. During this time the love of friends and family had assumed a greater importance in her life than previously, reinforcing her decision to stay in The Crossing.

Bypassing the main doors, she entered her own domain, smiling proudly to herself as her satisfied gaze swept round the practical but tastefully furnished office.

'Mine,' she thought as she closed the door behind her. 'All mine.' Being her own boss sure beat being a tiny cog in a huge corporate machine. Even with a hefty mortgage hanging over her head.

Comfortably seated behind her desk, she reached for the phone to investigate Jonathon Armitage's references. For her father's sake, definitely not her own she resolutely assured herself, she hoped they'd prove satisfactory. Her father was fretting about letting his customers down. Getting his garage up and running again would undoubtedly aid his recovery.

"Jon Armitage? Sure, he worked for me back awhile. Good bloke alright. Knows his stuff and can be trusted to do an honest day's work with no trouble. If you want a reliable mechanic, Jon's your man. Bit of a loner though, you know. Didn't stay long. Don't know what else I can tell you love."

"Thank you, Mr Goodwin."

Megan pursed her lips, thinking hard as she hung up the phone on the last of her random selection of Jon's past employers who had all said much the same.

Frowning, she balanced her need against the fact that although each of them had praised his technical skill, his honesty and his reliability, one serious drawback had emerged from the interviews.

A drawback which in view of the temporary nature of the job, probably wasn't all that relevant, she finally persuaded herself.

Jonathon Armitage was a drifter.

Since he'd finished his apprenticeship, the longest he'd spent in any job was a bare twelve months; usually eight months or less. No wonder the temporary nature of this job hadn't fazed him.

With that record he'd probably found it an added attraction!

Glancing at her watch, she saw she had time for a quick lunch and a change of clothes. There were several afternoon appointments in her diary and she liked to present a professional appearance in front of clients, even if most were old friends as well. The tatty jeans and football jersey she'd worn for weeding her father's garden that morning would never do.

Her inner voice, once again sounding way too much like her friend Geni, suggested it was a great pity she hadn't given herself time to change earlier.

Before Jonathon Armitage had caught her looking her absolute and utter worst.

Feeling the uncomfortable vibes of an undefined danger in that direction, Megan banished the dratted man from her mind and raced through the connecting door into her home and up the stairs.

Hurrying through the shower, her thoughts returned to the leather clad stranger. He was far and away the most attractive man Megan had seen since returning to Oxley Crossing.

When she had first left home, shortly before her eighteenth birthday, The Crossing had been in a slump. There'd been no future here for her, so she'd gone to Sydney to take up a traineeship with an accounting firm, attending university at night. Following this, she worked at the Taxation Office while furthering her studies.

Her feet firmly planted on her chosen career ladder, she had won several promotions, deservedly anticipating a successful climb to the top. Then had come her mother's illness and her return to The Crossing.

During her absence, there had been changes. Changes which had gone largely unnoticed on her fleeting visits to her parents. Tourists wandering off the beaten track had discovered the natural beauty of the region, and at the same time there had been an upturn in the economy.

Spurred on by the enthusiasm of the new owners of the old pub near the Morgan's Creek bridge, the local community had rushed to capitalise on fresh opportunities.

New, cautiously prosperous businesses had opened and farmers, the backbone of any rural community, had also prospered. Several good seasons combined with rural diversification had allowed them to enter lucrative new niche markets in addition to their traditional pursuits.

These days they were a progressive lot west of The Divide and The Crossing had embraced the future with buoyant optimism.

Opening her own office, Megan had committed herself to staying in her hometown, among people she loved and was comfortable with. So far, she'd had no cause to regret it. There was more than enough work to ensure her a comfortable living, and she was enjoying her independence and the quieter pace after the hustle and bustle of Sydney.

Rapidly flicking a brush through her short hair, she wondered what Jonathon Armitage was making of her town, then chastised herself for thinking of him. Again. Stubbornly resisting banishment, his image persistently returned to the forefront of her mind.

"No." Megan addressed her reflection in the bathroom mirror. "I am *not* preening for Jonathon Armitage." Playing with fire had never appealed to her.

Although he stirred her senses, a nomadic lone wolf like him was too dangerous for her peace of mind.

'Apart from his being clearly not interested,' she reminded herself, recalling his chilly indifference that morning.

However, since he'd already seen her at her worst in her old gardening clothes, it couldn't do her ego any harm to let him see how much more attractive she looked when she applied herself.

Although it would be even better if she could evict him from her mind entirely.

Her short, layered hairstyle lent an elfin quality to her heart-shaped face and her blue suit enhanced the blue of her eyes. A soft, silky blouse clung lovingly to small breasts and her grandmother's antique sapphire and seed pearl brooch provided the perfect finishing touch to her professional image.

She'd do. Nodding approval at her reflection, Megan left the room.

~~~~~

'Take a look around, the woman said. That should take five minutes, tops.'

Jon glanced at his watch. A little after eleven thirty.

'I'll give her until one o'clock to make her phone calls and reach a decision. It's only a temporary job for a motor mechanic, not some high-powered executive position.

If she can't give me an answer by then, I'll hit the road; and to hell with the job, and Oxley Crossing as well.'

Thinking about Megan Patterson brought that tingling sensation back to his hand. Irritated all over again, he made a mental note to check the electrics in the garage before starting work there.

Thinking about Megan Patterson also engendered a stirring in an altogether different portion of his anatomy. Snarling at himself in disgust he kicked sharply at an inoffensive pebble. Just because he'd felt her eyes on him while he filled up didn't mean he had to take any notice of her.

She'd had a nice enough face when he'd finally got a look at her, but she was nothing to write home about. Nothing to get him all steamed up. Especially if she always dressed in the sort of rags she was wearing this morning. There was no place in his life for a woman anyway.

Women were bad news.

Leaving the Harley where it was, he wandered back down Bridge Street. *'Appropriately named,'* he sneered, since it led up from the bridge. Opposite were sporting fields, the centrepiece of which was an old-fashioned grandstand. Signs pointing down a lane proclaimed the existence of a swimming pool and a golf course, and bordering the creek was an attractive park which would be as pleasant a spot as any to do his waiting. First though, he'd do as he'd been instructed, and look around. It was one way to fill in the time, after all.

Bypassing an 1890's bank building barricaded by painters' scaffolding, he entered an antique shop. His mother had collected antiques, and he'd acquired a rudimentary knowledge.

"Nice piece, that."

Jon swung round to find the proprietor at his elbow, nodding to the lovely old dresser he'd been studying.

"The name's Len. Len Woodcock." Jon shook the proffered hand.

"Yeah, it's not bad. Bit too big to strap on the back of the bike though."

To his surprise, he'd found the contents of the shop were of consistently high quality, and he easily used up the next half an hour chatting to Len while browsing around.

Moving right along, grudgingly admiring the turn-of-the-century lead light shop fronts and iron lace balconies, he stopped to study the window of the 'Oxley Crafts & Art Gallery'.

'Art gallery!'

Jon scoffed, but with time to waste, he sauntered through the door.

19

As he'd expected he found mostly the cottage craft. The style of things women liked to clutter up their homes with, although there was a display of pottery that took his fancy and some fine pieces of leather work.

Upstairs in the gallery he was surprised to find, not only the usual amateurish daubs attributed to local artists which he'd been expecting, but a rather impressive collection bearing the signatures of a number of reputable, well known Australian artists.

"Oxley Crossing's fast becoming the place to go to for decent bargains in art and antiques," the sales woman said when he commented on the collection.

"The lower rents out here mean we can be really competitive with city prices. People like to take a weekend getaway where they can pick up a bargain to boast about to their friends."

Impressed in spite of himself, Jon sauntered on, past a stock and station agency on the corner diagonally facing a modern supermarket behind an original Art Deco facade.

Further up this street, Peel Street, he saw signs announcing a butcher, hairdresser, dress shop, post office and police station. Maybe a couple of months here would be tolerable, but that would be the limit. No longer.

He was already counting the days till his departure.

Continuing down Bridge Street, a tummy rumble reminded him it was lunch time, prompting him to enter a bakery whose adjoining courtyard furnished with tables and chairs under bright umbrellas, was already almost full. He wandered in to see if there was anything decent on offer.

A frantically busy young Asian woman who managed to be everywhere at once, served him take-away coffee and a roll from an appetising, up-market range of pastries and breads.

Taking his lunch across to the park, Jon looked back up Bridge Street from 'The Victoria Inn', the historic pub next to the creek, to the service station.

Two blocks; that's all there was. And only one side street, with a generous scattering of houses covering the slope beyond the business area. His eyes took in the freshly furbished streetscape where gaily painted tubs spilling fragrant flowers lined the footpaths created a welcoming ambience.

But not welcoming enough to sway Jonathon Armitage. *'Definitely Hicksville,'* he sneered, reluctant to allow himself to admit to actually liking anything about Oxley Crossing.

Idly he wondered how much of a difference the tourists the gallery owner had mentioned made to the economy in a place like this. But his pay packet being the only economic factor he need concern himself with, Jon dismissed the town and its economy and sank hungry teeth into his roll. Some time later he glanced at his watch again.

'Time to check in with the Patterson woman.'

~~~~~

Back in her office with the computer booted up and files laid out neatly, ready for her afternoon appointments, Megan was the perfect picture of a prosperous businesswoman when Jon arrived. His face registered surprise on reading the sign on her door.

"So you're also an accountant! Pumping gas a sideline, is it?" he half sneered in lieu of a greeting, maintaining his cool impassivity when faced with the change in her appearance, but only just.

Dressed as she now was, without the camouflaging jersey, he could see she possessed a trim figure that was all woman. Subtly desirable woman.

He gave her long, slender legs another oh-so-casual glance. *'Not to my taste,'* he reminded himself, ignoring the involuntary tightening in his groin which asserted the opposite, *'but not too bad.'*

"I've been pumping gas on and off since I was a child," Megan replied casually, casting him an assessing glance. "Today, Jack needed an hour off, so I filled in."

Explanation over, she turned the conversation to the business at hand.

"I've checked your references," she stated, "and they're satisfactory as long as nobody wants your services long term."

She paused to give him an admonishing glance which was met by a bored looking stare giving nothing away.

Realising she wasn't going to be graced by any kind of explanatory comment, she continued smoothly as if unaware of being stonewalled.

"Since I expect Dad to be back on deck in a few months, that oughtn't to be a problem. I've prepared a contract, standard industry pay-rates plus overtime, five-and-a-half-day-week. Take a look at it, and if you're satisfied you can give me the details I need to calculate your pay and tax, etc."

Pleased with her brisk professional manner that countered the excited flutter in her solar region, Megan attempted to gauge his reaction.

Equally impersonal and businesslike, Jon read through the contract, filled in the information she required, and signed it.

"When do you want me to start?" he asked, his brusque tone grating on Megan's nerves. "Today's Friday. Will Monday be soon enough?"

"Monday will be fine." Relieved to have the worrying matter settled, Megan held out her hand for the customary shake on the deal.

Jon shook Megan's hand and felt that odd charge again. They were nowhere near the garage now, so he surmised it had to do with the woman, not the location.

If only he knew what caused it, he'd make damned sure he never gave it a chance to happen again. He was getting tired of being zapped every time Megan Patterson touched him.

Although the thought of having those small, soft, neatly manicured hands touch him more intimately, minus the electric shock, was a possibility that sent his imagination into overdrive.

Realising the direction his thoughts had strayed in, Jon abruptly wrenched them back into line.

He'd immediately recognised in Megan Patterson one of those women who took sexual affairs too seriously for comfort. His comfort, at any rate, since tying himself down featured nowhere in his future plans. Ever.

Megan Patterson was most definitely not his type, and therefore strictly off limits, even if she did stir his libido.

Smiling, thinking that the peculiar tingle really wasn't so scary after all, rather exciting in fact, Megan escorted Jon to the door, recommending he take a room at the hotel.

"It's really the only place in town with decent accommodation. Besides, Marge Morris is a terrific cook," she informed him.

About to exit Megan's office, Jon was almost bowled over by the young woman from the bakery who bustled in, calling out staccato apologies as she burst through the door.

"I'm late. So sorry Megan. Too many customers today. I couldn't get away on time."

Running speculative eyes over the tall, frowning man in black bike leathers, she raised an eyebrow, silently questioning the sexy stranger's presence.

"Elizabeth Tan; Jonathon Armitage." Happy to satisfy her friend's curiosity, Megan introduced them. "Elizabeth, you'll be very pleased to know Jon's our new mechanic. Jon, Elizabeth and her husband Jeff own the bakery, and Jeff's parents have the supermarket," she filled them both in.

"New mechanic, huh. So now I can get my car back. You got time to do it today? Then I can go see my mother tomorrow." Elizabeth looked expectantly at Jon. Megan explained.

"Elizabeth's car is in the workshop, Jon. Dad was working on it when he had his heart attack. He's been worrying about it ever since; and so has Elizabeth. I understand there's about an hour's work left to finish it."

"So, it's only just after lunch. Hours and hours left today. You can finish it now, then," Elizabeth stated triumphantly.

Weakly, Jon heard himself agreeing.

"As long as it's okay with Megan," he qualified. It was. Megan was more than happy to accommodate her friend.

"I'll give Jack O'Hara a call and he'll let you into the workshop and show you around," she informed him brightly.

'So much for starting Monday!'

Megan offered an apologetic smile to her new mechanic, but refused to feel guilty. Elizabeth had been very understanding about her car's extra-long pit stop and Jon would earn himself a little unexpected overtime. A win-win situation all round in her book.

Leaving Jon on the doorstep, the two women entered the office, closing the door behind them.

'Well, that settles my afternoon. Might as well go and get started. No need to rush to book a room at the hotel since I doubt they're overrun with guests.'

Ambling back next door to the service station, Jon steeled himself to beard Jack O'Hara in his den. Unless he'd been mistaken earlier, Jack was one old codger who hadn't exactly taken an instant shine to him.

'No matter,' Jon shrugged, *'I'm not in a popularity contest.'* As long as he did his work properly, no-one would have cause to complain.

SAVING JONATHON ARMITAGE

3

Forewarned by the bush telegraph, Marge Morris had prepared a quiet room away from the noisy public area for Jon. While she settled him in she regaled him with a running commentary on the town's history and current attractions.

She and her husband Phil were doing all they could to put Oxley Crossing on the tourist map, even going so far as to build a small block of motel units and a miniature caravan park behind the hotel anticipating that their trickle of visitors would become an influx.

They had also been instrumental in developing some of the area's natural attractions.

"You'll find lots to do while you're here, Jon." Warmly enthusiastic, Marge, a comfortably plump middle-aged matron patted her bouffant blonde waves.

"In fact, you probably won't want to leave when the time comes." She laughed genteelly at her own well-practised joke, ignoring Jon's non-committal grunt.

"We've constructed an all-weather walking and jogging track along the creek where you might be lucky enough to see the rare regent honeyeater, and there are several scenic drives. You'll find the country around here very pretty, especially where we've built some nice little picnic spots and lookouts."

Barely pausing for breath, she wound up her spiel by pressing an information brochure into his hands, then left him to unpack in peace.

A quick job when all his worldly goods were crammed into a bantam-sized bike trailer and a couple of saddle-bags.

Showered and changed into comfortable, well-worn jeans and a clean shirt, Jon sat morosely in the room's single armchair and flicked through the brochure. *'Yeah, there's lots to do all right; a couple of hours on the bike and I could see it all in half a day.'* Town amenities were listed on the back.

Plenty of sporting clubs as he'd already noticed, only he wasn't a joiner and didn't plan to stay that long anyway. The library. Now that was something he could use, especially since he didn't anticipate a busy social life during the next couple of months. He'd look in there in the morning and see if they had anything worth reading.

Hearing the hall clock chime the hour, Jon dragged himself out of the armchair and went in search of the dining room.

The first decent meal he'd enjoyed in days mellowed his mood considerably.

Marge Morris was a terrific cook; the Patterson woman had got that right.

Tired of his own company, Jon sauntered into the bar in search of entertainment, finding it in a light-hearted flirtation with Angie Wilson, the pretty, young, red-haired barmaid who, according to Marge, also lived in the hotel.

The voluptuous Angie came on strong, but Jon suspected it was her professional patter rather than genuine interest in himself. *'Better keep it light,'* he advised himself. *'In a small town, I could end up in big trouble if I'm not careful.'* And he'd learned the hard way to be a careful man.

With this warning to himself, he left Angie behind the bar and strolled into the next room to knock a few balls around on the pool table.

"Hey mate, care for a game? Ten bucks on the side."

"Sure, why not?" A bland expression disguising satisfaction, Jon accepted. He'd made a few dollars in the past, playing pool, and with the security of a job, could afford to risk the meagre change remaining in his wallet. A few curious spectators gathered to watch.

The first game went to Jon and soon there was a noisy queue of hopefuls lining up to challenge the newcomer. With a nice run of luck Jon raked in enough to pay his bar tab with a satisfying windfall left over.

When Phil Morris called for last drinks, Jon's pockets were sufficiently well-lined for him to shout his erstwhile opponents a round in compensation for their losses; a move guaranteeing immediate acceptance from the locals.

~~~~~

Saturday was obviously not the busy day of the week, Jon concluded as he went looking for the library the next morning, finding it down Peel Street in a restored federation cottage beyond the Community Hall. More fresh paint and flowers.

What was it with this town, anyway? He wasn't used to such a profusion of well-tended public gardens everywhere he looked.

"You must be Jonathon Armitage."

Edith Turner, the librarian, already familiar with Jon's name via the bush telegraph, beamed up at him when he fronted her desk.

"I'm so glad you found your way into my library. I've been hearing good things about you, young man, and was hoping to meet you soon." She was more than happy to issue him with a temporary membership card.

Making the most of her opportunity, she quizzed him gently, then left him to look about on his own. Around the end of a stack in the well-stocked little library, he came face to face with an all too familiar figure.

One that caused his pulse to race in a disconcerting manner.

Megan Patterson appeared cool and casual and more attractive than he remembered, in hip-hugging white denim shorts and a dark red halter top that earned her a thorough survey from those brooding eyes.

"Why, hello Jon. Settled in, are you?"

'And how banal is that!'

Megan chided herself for wishing to impress the man who'd invaded her dreams the night before. Invaded them against her wishes, and her better judgement.

Oh, why couldn't she simply relegate him to some tiny, unimportant corner on the far distant periphery of her life where he belonged?

Why was she so ambivalent? Why did all her good intentions melt into oblivion as soon as the dratted man came within touching distance?

Well, this time at least she had an unimpeachable reason to approach him, so she'd make the most of her opportunity, dangerous or not.

Nodding, Jon was about to pass by with no more than a muttered "Morning Megan," when she stepped into the middle of the aisle deliberately blocking his all too obvious desire to escape.

Pretending to notice neither, she smiled warmly into his eyes.

Jon felt his heart sink and his stomach clench and braced himself to repel the advances of this woman he wanted but knew he couldn't have. Only to be confronted by an innocence he found infinitely more difficult to resist.

"I'm so glad we met this morning, Jon. I really do appreciate your good nature, fixing Elizabeth's car like that yesterday."

Afraid she may have pre-judged Jon unfairly, Megan had decided to give him the benefit of the doubt.

Besides, since he was here for a while wouldn't it only be common sense to be friendly?

'*Especially to a young, single man who makes me want things I've never wanted before?*' her Geni sounding inner voice added snidely.

Danger be damned.

Bravely, she sucked in a deep, much needed breath and reached out to take his hands, daring the curious spark that set her heart racing.

"Elizabeth's very grateful too," Megan continued. "You could easily have left her car till Monday; only you didn't. Thank you, Jon."

She squeezed gently, then meeting with no response other than a deprecating nod she was left with no option except to reluctantly drop his hands when what she really wanted was to explore the feel of their work-roughened texture against her own softer skin.

About to take her leave of him, she recalled another snippet she could pass on, thereby prolonging their encounter.

"By the way Jon, I phoned all the people who've been waiting to have work done. You'll find the details in the work schedule. You have a pretty full week ahead of you."

"Busy's what I prefer," he answered, cool and unsmiling.

Megan hesitated, but, was forced to accept that Jon was a man of few words. She really should have known better than to play the femme fatale, a role she knew didn't suit her. Defeated, she backed away a couple of steps.

"One evening when you've got time to spare," she finished up with a now strained gaiety, "Dad would like to meet you. He's back in our local cottage hospital."

About to move away, she turned back to add, "Visiting hours are six till eight each evening." Another warm smile and a quick, "Bye Jon. See you around," and she was gone.

Jon released a pent-up breath. Although annoyed at the unwanted effect Megan's nearness had had on him, he couldn't help wondering what she was doing for the rest of the day.

He quickly suppressed the insidious little whisper in the back of his mind that said Megan Patterson might be good company on one of those scenic rides, remembering in the nick of time that she wasn't his kind of woman, before he ran after her to ask.

Hastily chosen books in hand, a new murder mystery, a biography and a travel story that looked interesting, Jon wandered back to the hotel, stopping to buy a few basic necessities on his way.

Now what? A whole weekend stretched endlessly in front of him, begging to be filled. What did people around here do for entertainment on the weekend?

One thing he could do, he decided, was to thoroughly check out the garage. Yesterday he'd been busy, all the tools he needed still lying on the trolley beside Elizabeth's car. He hadn't spent much time looking round.

This morning he would see what Old Man Patterson had in the way of tools and equipment, and where it was all stored; rearrange it a little to suit himself, perhaps.

At least it would fill in a couple of hours, probably saving him time next week, when according to Megan Patterson he was going to be busy.

Acting impulsively on his decision, he headed for the garage.

"Morning Jack."

Jon relished the surprise on the older man's face.

"Bit early, aren't yer? Didn't think I'd be seein' you again till Monday morning."

Jack tugged on the corner of his moustache, eyeing Jon suspiciously.

Taking pity on him, Jon explained as he helped himself to the workshop key.

"I thought it'd be a good idea to check everything out thoroughly before I get too busy."

He wasn't entirely sure, but he thought he saw a faint glimmer of respect creep into Jack's eyes before the man turned away from him to serve a customer.

Actually, Old Man Patterson ran a pretty tight ship. The equipment and tools were beautifully maintained and all stored in convenient, clearly labelled spots with a sufficient range of tools and spare parts to handle any job likely to come his way.

It flashed through Jon's mind that it could be very rewarding, owning a tidy little business like this one. But he shut that impossible dream down fast.

In the past, every time he'd tried to create a niche for himself, he'd botched his chances. Now he simply accepted he wasn't suited to a settled existence and left it at that. Hastily, he directed his thoughts elsewhere.

Satisfied, he knew he would quickly be able to lay his hands on any item he might need.

He was on the point of leaving when Jack elbowed the door open, a fragrantly steaming mug of coffee in each hand.

"Not sure how yer take it," he rumbled. "There's milk and sugar back there if you want 'em. Biscuits too. Help yerself."

Thanking him and assuring the older man that straight up was how he preferred his coffee, Jon followed him out the back door into the garden. If Jack O'Hara was prepared to be friendly, he'd meet him halfway. It was no skin off his nose and would make working here a lot more pleasant.

"Nice garden, this un," Jack commented. "Mike's pride and joy, it is. That there's a useful shady spot for a break." He nodded towards a charming rose arbour. "Mike don't mind if we take our breaks out here."

They sat alongside each other on a garden seat, shiny from frequent use, and Jack set himself to dredge as much information as he could out of the younger man. He was a skilled interrogator, but Jonathon Armitage proved to be equally skilled at evading personal questions.

Coffee finished, a disgruntled Jack took the empty mugs and wandered off.

~~~~~

Despite Jon's depressing lack of response, Megan had detoured to take a quick peep in the mirror in the children's corner of the library.

'*Scowl at me he might,*' she thought, her nerve ends still tingling from the brief encounter, '*but he also looked me over from head to toe. Thoroughly.*'

No, nothing was out of place. She looked as good as she ever did.

'Not that that's saying much,' she told herself glumly, unaware others saw in her face a liveliness and charm unapparent to herself when dourly studying her reflection in the mirror. Her excitement doused by that sobering thought, she wandered off to collect her books. Taking them to be stamped, she exchanged friendly greetings with Edith.

Pushing her Dame Edna style glasses high onto an aquiline nose with a bony finger, Edith impaled Megan with a piercing stare.

"I reckon he's a lost soul, your Jonathon Armitage," she said, surprising Megan.

"I think all that surly, loner stuff is just camouflage; a pose to hide his true feelings. But you know something, Meggie, if we get enough time to work at it, we may be able to save him. I think he's worth the effort."

"You could be right, Eddie, except he's not *my* Jonathon Armitage, and I don't believe we have any right to interfere in his personal life," Megan retorted sharply.

Ego smarting from being given the cold shoulder for the second time, she strenuously resisted her misplaced interest in the dratted man.

Edith's heart was in the right place, she knew, but good grief; imagine the trouble a girl could get into trying to 'save' a man like Jonathon Armitage!

Who would save her if she was foolish enough to get involved with him?

A good-looking, experienced man like Jon, an irresponsible drifter to boot, was way out of her league, exciting though she found him. Megan preferred a man with roots in his community; a man she could trust to be there for her; a man who would love only her.

Yet, although she knew Jon was all wrong for her, at this moment Megan wished she was more like her friend Geni.

If Geni was attracted to a man as Megan was to Jon, she'd throw caution to the wind and follow her heart.

To her consternation, Megan felt herself blushing, excitement building all over again as she recalled the odd tingle she'd experienced each time she'd made physical contact with Jon.

It hadn't been at all unpleasant. Quite the reverse. In fact, on reflection, she found there was something rather heart-warming about it. Would it happen again?

She almost giggled aloud thinking maybe she should conduct an experiment to find out.

'Shame on you, Megan Patterson,' she reprimanded herself. It must be Geni's influence rubbing off on her. She ought to know better.

She did know better.

~~~~~

Strolling back to The Victoria for lunch, Jon's attention was caught by the increased volume of traffic now filling the street. It was a sunny weekend and it seemed a slew of intrepid tourists were out and about.

Most of the parking spaces were occupied and a coach was waiting over by the park. Had he misjudged the attractions of the place?

Shrugging impatiently, he considered how to fill the afternoon, deciding finally to follow one of the drives on Marge's brochure.

There was a mountain to climb, a whole six hundred and thirty-eight metres, he noted, scanning the text. Some mountain! It offered panoramic views of the entire countryside. Not that he was optimistic enough to imagine he'd see much different from on his ride into town. Bush was bush.

Returning, he could visit an Aboriginal art site. Might be better than lounging around the hotel with a book all afternoon, he supposed.

It was to be hoped there wouldn't be many more dreary weekends like this before he made his escape from this godforsaken hole!

Life always felt better on the back of a bike, the wind whistling past his ears. When Angie picked up her light-hearted flirtation where she'd left off the evening before, he offered her the pillion seat on the Harley; not unduly upset when she declined.

"Sorry, but I have to work, Jon," she explained. "Maybe some other time."

So much for that.

Jon wasn't interested in Angie, it was simply that he was bored with his own company. She might have provided an entertaining diversion.

That evening Jon found the hotel well patronised by visitors breaking their weekend getaways in Oxley Crossing. Unfortunately for him, they'd kept to themselves and the locals were conspicuous by their absence. According to Angie, Friday was the big night out for the locals. When their pub was full of outsiders they looked for entertainment elsewhere.

Jon refused to admit to himself that his boredom was rooted in loneliness. Television in the lounge filled the time until he could reasonably take himself off to bed, but tonight he'd found television a poor substitute for human company.

Sunday looked like being another long, boring day for Jon until he saw there was a cricket match across on the oval, and wandered over to fill in an hour or two.

"Hey there, Armitage. The home team supporters sit over here. Take a pew."

Looking up, Jon recognised one of his challengers from Friday night and sat down in the space he and his mates offered. His heart warmed as he was introduced around. This was a gratifying new experience, being included in community activities as if he belonged.

Usually he just hung out with whatever other unattached, itinerant blokes he came across. His spirits lifted, bringing a spontaneous smile to his lips.

From her spot further along the benches, Megan's mouth dropped open in surprise.

Minus the scowl, Jon Armitage looked a whole different man. The hidden man whose existence Eddie had intuited? This new man bore watching. He represented uncounted possibilities.

Jon had met several of the players and spectators in the bar on Friday night, so he settled down comfortably to enjoy himself.

A stranger, casually introducing himself as Alan Morgan, thrust an icy can of coke into Jon's hand and dropped onto the seat beside him. He'd just ended a dashing batting partnership by getting caught in the slips, and the two of them talked desultorily while watching the progress of the game. Jon was pleasantly surprised to discover he had more in common with the rugged young farmer than he would have imagined.

If he got to spend his spare time in company like this, the couple of months he was stuck here mightn't be too unbearable.

Over lunch he found himself one of a crowd of young people, inordinately disappointed that Megan Patterson, another familiar face in the crowd, kept to the other end of the set of tables.

He knew she wasn't his type of woman, but she was the only woman he'd met in Oxley Crossing he felt the urge to spend time with.

As the lunch break was finishing the conversation turned to community affairs. Alan Morgan was asking Megan something about a bank opening.

Listening idly, Jon discovered they were talking about the building where Megan had her office. A building she apparently owned.

Not only that, it seemed Megan had also been the driving force behind the town's being accorded the new bank branch about to be opened.

Helping her own financial position, she had fortunately been able to lease most of the remodelled business floor to the new community bank, retaining a separate, smaller office suite for herself.

Quite a coup for someone so young. Jon felt a humbling respect for his lady boss that almost doused the physical response the sight of her had aroused in him. Almost.

It helped his self-control that when he arrived she'd given him a wave and a cheerful "Hi Jon", then ignored him.

He wasn't aware of her eyes tracking him when he wasn't looking, or of her almost irresistible urge to sit down beside him and claim his company for herself

If he had been, he might have given in to the aching need to get her to himself, far away from the crowd watching the cricket match.

Megan was fending off some good-natured teasing about owning the bank, laughingly reminding them that her ownership was limited to the heavily mortgaged building that housed the bank.

A girl whose name Jon couldn't remember, joked that the way she was going, Megan would be a millionaire before she was thirty.

"Well Sophie," Megan laughed, rebuffing the prediction, "that would certainly be nice, only I'm a long, looong way short of that target, and since I'll be twenty-eight next birthday, I'm running out of time."

'Twenty-eight! She doesn't look it,' Jon thought.

Dressed casually in short shorts and sleeveless knit top, Megan looked barely twenty. Instead she was closer to his own thirty-two.

Anyway, why was he wasting time thinking about Megan Patterson?

Being a prosperous, self-employed accountant was more than enough to put her way out of the league of a simple grease monkey for hire. One who's sole tangible asset was his Harley.

Pity though. Eyeing Megan's long, slender legs Jon felt a renewed stirring in his loins.

4

Megan, smartly dressed in another short-skirted business suit that drew his eyes to those delectable slender legs, was waiting for Jon on Monday morning.

She greeted him with one of her warm smiles, setting his imagination aflame with 'what ifs' and 'if onlys'. Impossibilities he had trouble dragging his mind, and his rebellious body, away from. But apparently her purpose was not pleasure, so taking a deep, steadying breath, he forced himself to concentrate on business.

"I'll just run you through the paperwork, Jon, and give you the ordering codes so you can send away for parts when you need them," she said. It was all standard procedure; forms Jon was familiar with.

Seeing this, Megan concluded quickly. She was afraid to dawdle in this man's company.

He aroused thoughts of pleasures which, if pursued, she feared would leave her a shattered wreck when he left.

As she knew he would.

Jonathon Armitage was too dangerous to her peace of mind, but how she wished it could be otherwise. Giving herself a mental shake, she quickly concluded the business that had necessarily placed her in his orbit this morning.

"Anyway Jon," she reminded him, "if a problem does crop up, you know where to find me."

'Or even if there isn't a problem,' whispered her unruly inner voice.

His first customer arriving just then, she patted him on the arm and left him to get on with it. He didn't see her cheeky grin because her back was to him.

When opportunity offered, Megan hadn't been able to resist conducting her experiment after all. The result?

The peculiar electricity was definitely exclusive to Jonathon Armitage. She'd carried out the same test on several other men yesterday at the cricket match, not one of them producing a similar effect on her.

Only Jonathon.

Intriguing.

Although it completely passed her understanding. Did he have that effect on everyone, or just her?

Thinking back, she remembered it had taken him by surprise during their first meeting. The realisation it was exclusive to the *two* of them left her feeling positively light-headed.

~~~~~

Long after Megan left the garage, Jon continued to feel the imprint of her hand on his arm. The scent of her spicy floral perfume lingered in the dusty air, invoking her smiling image in his mind.

He had noted Megan's smile more than once. Sweet and warm, it reflected her genuine interest in the person she bestowed it on. Megan's smile lit up her face all the way to her eyes, warming the heart of its recipient.

Even Jon's, soured as it was by disillusionment, began dreaming of the impossible when she turned its power on him. And Megan smiled often.

'Damn it all, Armitage. Can't you get your mind off the bloody woman?' he berated himself. *'There's too much work to waste time mooning over a woman's smile.'* Picking up a spanner, he applied himself to the job in hand with dogged determination.

Today, Jon was finding it difficult to remember why Megan Patterson wasn't his type.

Lunch break almost over, he was enjoying the sunshine in the garden, when a heavily-built, grey haired man in a police sergeant's uniform strolled through the back door.

"Don Matthews. Guess you must be Jon Armitage. Good to meet you."

He reached out to shake hands. Guilelessly, he watched for Jon's reaction before sitting alongside him.

'Good enough,' thought Don.

The young chap had looked him straight in the eye without the slightest hint of shiftiness. In excess of twenty years on the force meant Don could tell when someone was uncomfortable around police officers; and this fellow was okay.

Of course, he'd already run him through the police computers as a favour to Mike, and he'd come out clean. Some unpleasant business in the fellow's life though, to give him that dark, haunted look at the back of his eyes. However, Don would swear it didn't involve the law.

Satisfied, the sergeant got on with the excuse he had used as an opportunity to check out the new mechanic personally.

"Reason I looked in, Jon, I got this flyer a couple of days ago. Thought you wouldn't mind keeping an eye out for this mob. Let me know if they show up round here, won't you mate."

He handed Jon the flyer warning of a gang selling dodgy spare parts, then, clapping him on the shoulder, Sergeant Matthews took himself off again.

Wryly amused at having been looked over by the police, a procedure that was certainly not the norm, Jon went back to work.

Dinner over that evening, he decided to visit his new boss in the hospital, finding both Jack O'hara and Don Matthews there before him.

Once they had tactfully left, Mike Patterson got down to business, grilling Jon thoroughly about his training and experience. Mike trusted his daughter, but Megan didn't know the trade and might have been bluffed by a fancy set of papers without substance to back them up.

Visiting hours over, Jon left, confident he'd managed to satisfy the old man his customers and their vehicles were safe in his hands.

~~~~~

From her kitchen window, Megan could see Jon when he took his breaks in her father's garden. It annoyed her that repeated attempts to wipe him from her mind had failed abysmally. His virile masculinity evoked a wholly new and exciting feminine response in her. A response she longed to explore further, but, warned off by the icy reserve in Jon's eyes when he looked at her, she reminded herself she couldn't afford to let it go to her head.

Besides, news travelled fast in a small town, and Megan knew who Jon was spending his evenings flirting with. Maybe more, if the rumours around town were to be believed.

Angie Wilson.

Megan had avoided The Victoria in recent months, her usual self-confidence unusually threatened by Angie's voluptuous beauty and blatant sexuality. Normally comfortable with her own lesser charms, next to Angie, she became depressed by awareness of what she perceived to be her own inadequacies.

If that was the kind of woman Jon wanted, and apparently it was, she wasn't even in the competition. '*Let him stick to Angie Wilson then,*' Megan thought with an uncharacteristic spurt of jealousy.

Even so, irresistibly drawn to Jon like Yogi Bear to a picnic basket, Megan found herself creating a reason to seek him out yet again.

Walking up to him in the garden, resolutely ignoring the 'Keep off' signals flashing from his eyes, Megan lay her hand on top of Jon's where it rested on the table. Revelling in the feel of its hard strength she imagined those work-roughened hands caressing her skin.

Secretly enjoying her daring, a pleasurable shiver rippled up her spine. Enjoying also the warmth of their peculiar electricity.

Surely something so strange and particular must hold special significance? Raising deliberately innocent blue eyes to Jon's shadowed grey orbs, Megan spoke from her heart.

"Thanks for looking in on Dad so promptly, Jon. You have no idea how much you relieved his mind. Hearing what a mystery man you are, he'd been getting a bit worked up." *'And wasn't that an understatement!'*

Slanting a sidelong glance Jon's way, she flashed him a complicit grin, willing him to open up to her; not at all surprised when he didn't rise to the bait. She was beginning to understand this difficult man, just a little. Undaunted, she pressed on.

"Having met you himself, Jon, he knows you're okay and has relaxed again." She flashed him another, even warmer, smile, thinking that holding a conversation with this aloof man was painfully arduous work.

'A worthless effort?' Her inner voice questioned. *'Never!'* Persevering, she tried again. "How are you getting on at the garage? No problems, I hope."

"Everything's okay. No problems," Jon muttered. Defeated, Megan gave up.

"Remember, anytime you want me, I'm right next door."

'If only,' she thought, realising her inadvertent double entendre.

'Why do I continue to be drawn towards the dratted man when he makes it clear he isn't interested in me? What makes him so different from other men that I'm failing so dismally to brush him aside and get on with my life?'

Really, Jonathon Armitage was a distraction she neither needed nor wanted. Or so she tried to convince herself.

Giving his hand another friendly pat, she took herself back to her own side of the fence before she made a fool of herself by revealing how much she was affected by that magnetic tug of raw energy when she touched his hand.

It had felt good, tempting her to take risks she had never taken before, even faced with his lack of encouragement.

~~~~~

'Me relieve Mike Patterson's mind!' Alone again, Jon almost snorted aloud at that. *'More likely,'* he thought, *'it was down to Jack O'Hara and Don Matthews making their reports.'*

God, he'd felt such a yokel just now. That damned wildfire energy flowing through him from Megan's hand lying on top of his own had addled his wits.

He'd had to fight so hard against the urge to grab her in his arms, he'd ended up so tongue-tied he could barely speak.

Jon couldn't understand what was wrong with him. No other woman had ever had this uncomfortable effect on him. He was more or less all right as long as Megan didn't touch him.

As soon as she lay her soft, shapely little hand on his arm, all his good intentions were blown away, leaving him wanting her in the worst possible way. Wanting her more each time. Wanting her even when she wasn't anywhere near him.

Was it simply because he'd declared her off limits? Too bad if it was. She was trouble, and he made it a rule to avoid trouble. Although, for some reason, Megan was harder to avoid than any woman he'd previously encountered.

Cursing savagely under his breath, Jon wished Megan would stay away from him.

She wasn't even his type, only he couldn't remember any longer quite what his type of woman was.

Megan Patterson's image kept clouding his vision.

5

Killing boredom, a morose Jonathon Armitage joined the handful of locals in the bar on Thursday night, keeping to Phil's end, as far as he could get from Angie. Her flirty manner had been amusing at first, but he'd about had enough of it.

Turning abruptly as a bony finger jabbed him in the shoulder, he came face to face with Edith Turner, the middle-aged librarian. He'd seen her at the cricket match, but other than a brief hello, hadn't spoken to her.

What could she want with him? Seemed like he was about to find out. With a resigned sigh, he greeted her politely.

"You're just the man I'm looking for," beamed Edith. "Jonathon Armitage, I need to talk to you. A shandy for me, please Phil, and another of whatever Jon's drinking for him."

With that, she dragged him off his comfortable bar-stool and over to a quiet corner table.

"I hope you don't mind, Jon, but I need your help," she began. Then not wasting a moment, and not giving Jon the tiniest opening to voice the protest teetering on his lips, Edith set to work.

Talking hard and fast, she compelled him with her earnest gaze. Before he knew quite how it happened, he found himself drafted into a working bee in the park. Mission accomplished, Edith left as speedily as she'd arrived, leaving a somewhat bemused young man staring after her.

'That sweet faced little woman is a human steam roller!'

Jon shook his head, stunned to realise he had just agreed to spend a whole Saturday afternoon working on the park's unfinished picnic facilities.

The gist of Edith's argument had appeared to be that she was the organiser for the Tidy Towns Competition, the judging of which was imminent, and the scheduled work unfinished. Mike Patterson had promised to help. Now Mike couldn't do it. Jon had stepped into Mike's shoes, so Edith reckoned it was up to Jon to fulfil Mike's commitment.

A spurious argument at best.

If only he'd thought a bit quicker. Unfortunately, Edith's mesmerising gaze had temporarily robbed him of his capacity for rational thought. Jon shrugged.

He'd given his word, so he supposed he'd have to keep it. *'Although,'* he reminded himself, *'I don't owe this town a damned thing!'*

Making a mental note to give Edith Turner a wide berth in future, Jon wandered upstairs to read in his room.

At least there he was safe from being roped into anything else.

~~~~~

The next evening, half-heartedly parrying Angie's lures, Jon was relieved to see Alan Morgan slide onto the stool next to him at the bar.

When the rising noise level generated by the Friday night crowd made conversation difficult, they adjourned to the pool tables for a friendly game.

Pleasantly surprised after a week of dull, quiet evenings, Jon realised later how much he'd enjoyed himself.

Alan was good company, and he played a challenging game of pool. Although Jon won by a narrow margin, it was a close-run contest; and the best entertainment he'd had for a while.

"Oh, well done Jon. I reckon you're the best player this town has seen for quite a while."

Angie had followed up her fulsome compliment with a swift peck on his cheek, something she'd never done before, then hurried off about her task of delivering orders and clearing away empty glasses.

Had her livelier than usual flirtatiousness with himself tonight had an ulterior purpose? Jon's narrowed eyes followed her suspiciously as he recalled several other similar incidents that evening.

It hadn't escaped his notice that she'd practically ignored Alan altogether.

Neither had he missed Alan's frowning, tight-lipped gaze surreptitiously tracking the redhead as she sashayed back and forth.

The uncomfortable suspicion he was being used settled in Jon's mind. From the first, he'd rated Angie Wilson as a potential problem, and her behaviour tonight seemed to confirm his assessment.

If she and Alan Morgan had unfinished business, he'd need to be particularly careful not to get caught in the middle.

Gorgeous though Angie was, she left him cold.

Unlike that damned long-legged witch of an accountant with her mysterious touch. *She* had the power to arouse him, even when absent! His arm tingled from the remembered echo of her personal electricity. If he hadn't been a thoroughly modern man he might have suspected witchcraft.

~~~~~

Down by the creek on Saturday afternoon, Jon stood looking around him.

A group of early arrivals had already begun work, several of whom he knew well enough to greet by name. There was Megan, one of a team of gardeners already busy weeding and planting seedlings; and there was Alan, assembling a picnic table.

And, yes, here came the indomitable Edith Turner bearing down on him with a purposeful air.

When he related the way she'd trapped him the other night, Alan had laughed.

"Watch your step around old Eddie Turner, mate," he'd warned him, snickering as if there was more he could have added but chose not to.

For a small woman Edith Turner had a great deal of presence.

In no time at all, she'd assigned Jon to Alan's team, which was okay by him.

Since he was stuck here for the afternoon he'd much prefer the company of a man he already knew and liked to that of a total stranger.

As the afternoon progressed, he relaxed. These Tidy Towners were an okay group, and he found himself enjoying working alongside them in the spring sunshine.

More and more often his eyes strayed of their own volition to where Megan knelt, leaning over garden beds to plant flower seedlings.

Her cute posterior clad in tight, red stretch shorts repeatedly caught his eye. Feeling himself becoming heated by more than the sun, Jon wished she'd move away, out of his line of sight. When his wish was granted, he was disgusted to find himself changing position to regain the enticing view.

With a self-conscious flush he turned his back, hoping his interest hadn't been obvious.

Megan had instantly noted Jon's arrival, mildly surprised to discover Edith had recruited him to the cause. She hadn't imagined Jon being interested in a community project such as this.

Until she remembered Edith's comments about 'saving' him, and grinned to herself.

Edith was a power to be reckoned with, as she knew from past experience. It could prove interesting to see how she fared with Jonathon Armitage.

And beneficial to herself? With a little help from Edith the impossible just might come within reach. Buoyed by renewed optimism, Megan blushed and began to feel all kinds of impossible things might not, after all, be truly impossible.

Throughout the afternoon she kept sneaking quick peeks, admiring the play of sweat-sheened muscles as Jon lifted roof trusses onto the picnic shelters and hammered down sheets of corrugated iron roofing.

The red bandana holding his hair back from his eyes emphasised the strong angles of his face, making Megan's hands itch uncharacteristically to caress those high-boned cheeks and wide brow.

When he'd tugged his T-shirt off, her eyes had opened wide, feasting greedily on the broad expanse of smooth suntanned skin, intrigued by the mat of dark chest hair swirling round flat brown nipples and arrowing below the waistband of his denim cut-offs, leading her eyes in that very interesting direction.

The discovery of a fierce little dragon tattooed high up on his left shoulder was almost her undoing. Of all the mythical creatures, dragons were her favourites. Desire washed over Megan in hot waves, even after she forced herself to look away.

'Why does he stir me like this?' She demanded of herself.

Other men, no matter how sexy or good looking they were, didn't arouse her to this degree, without even coming anywhere near her.

Embarrassed, she hoped no-one had noticed her absorption. Especially not Jonathon Armitage! Very sternly, she forbade herself to look at him again. Then promptly broke her new rule.

"Cuppa time," warbled Edith.

On the newly erected tables she'd set out a cooler of iced water and boiled the urn for tea and coffee. Tins of home-baked biscuits appeared next to the cups. Grateful for the break, her workers came drifting across to serve themselves.

Jon had no sooner eased himself onto a bench than, to his consternation, Megan slipped in beside him.

It would be too rude to move away from her, so Jon surrendered to the inevitable. Bare thighs and arms grazing, tingling warmly, he gritted his teeth, resigning himself to half an hour of torture.

Until he realised he was getting used to that peculiar reaction.

Concentrating, striving this time to understand it, he noticed how all his senses appeared heightened all of a sudden. The eucalyptus-scented air smelled fresher. The azure spring sky looked bluer. Magpies carolling for handouts sounded sweeter. Even Edith's home-baked Anzac biscuits tasted extra good.

Awed, Jon realised that with Megan Patterson pressed tightly against his side, he felt altogether more vividly alive.

Happy, with a contentment he'd almost forgotten, quite safe from temptation in full view of so many people, he relaxed, letting himself enjoy the sensation of Megan's body brushing sensuously against his own; letting himself enjoy her alluring spicy perfume teasing his nostrils.

The conversation flowed over him as he sat, idly entranced in pleasant daydreams.

When Megan joggled his elbow to attract his attention, he was jolted back into the present.

"Well, what about it Jon? Are you on?" Alan was addressing him. What had his question been?

Confused at being dragged so abruptly out of his pleasant reverie, Jon was forced to admit he hadn't been listening.

"Next Sunday, Jon," Alan repeated impatiently. "Will you be able to help me out at the picnic ground at Rainbow Falls? Barbecue at the farm afterwards." Mildly embarrassed at being caught daydreaming, Jon hastened to agree. Another of these Tidy Towns projects aimed at improving the tourist appeal of The Crossing, apparently.

"Good man Jon. You're exactly the civic minded type of citizen this town needs more of." Beaming, Edith nodded her approval across the table.

What was he getting himself into? Here he was, committed to yet another working bee next weekend. At least it filled in the time, Jon supposed, and the work wasn't difficult.

He might as well do something useful, rather than lounge about reading or watching television on his days off.

Was Megan going too, he wondered, suddenly interested. If she was, maybe he should offer her a lift on the Harley.

He'd need someone to show him the way, wouldn't he?

~~~~~

Long after she retired to bed that night, Megan was still able to feel the imprint of Jon's thigh pressed warmly against her own, his bare arm brushing against hers.

"He's coming with us next weekend, too," she whispered gleefully into the darkness. His scowls and black looks forgotten today, he had been a different, altogether more approachable, man. Maybe next weekend she'd be able to spend some time getting to know him even better.

Getting closer to him?

Giggling to herself, Megan realised she hadn't indulged in fantasies like these since she had been a very young girl with a crush on one of her teachers. That had painlessly faded to nothing when she met his wife and baby at a picnic day. Her subconscious voice proclaimed loudly that this attraction to Jon was a vastly different proposition, and she was forced to agree.

There was absolutely nothing childlike about the emotions and desires aroused by thoughts of Jonathon Armitage.

Maybe she should listen to her subconscious.

Maybe she should take up the challenge. It was said leopards couldn't change their spots, but Jon wasn't a leopard. So maybe he could give up his aimless wandering and settle down.

And didn't *that* idea spark off some intriguing possibilities! It was with a smile curving her lips that Megan finally fell asleep.

~~~~~

It was Wednesday lunchtime before Jon met up with Megan again. By then, he'd reversed his intention of offering her a ride on the Harley.

The attraction she held for him gave her the potential to become a serious impediment in his footloose lifestyle.

Megan Patterson was not a girl to be safely inveigled into a light affair, which was all he had to offer her. Therefore, Jon decided, he would do her a huge kindness and keep right out of her way.

In fact, he became so busy avoiding Megan, it escaped his notice how much time he spent watching for her comings and goings.

Humming merrily, Megan breezed into the rose arbour where Jon had taken his lunch. Perching herself on the seat beside him, she smiled cheerfully and began to speak before she was properly settled.

"Hi Jon. Now, about Sunday afternoon. If you'd like a lift, Angie and I are going with Bob, and there's room in his car for you as well."

She looked expectantly at him, waiting for an answer, smiling her pleasure when he accepted the ride.

There was safety in numbers, Jon consoled himself. Besides, his brain going into shutdown as usual in Megan's proximity, he hadn't been able to come up with any good reason to refuse.

"Be ready at twelve-thirty, then." Megan patted his shoulder and was gone as abruptly as she'd arrived.

Once safely back on her own side of the fence, she let the smile slip from her face to be replaced with a frown.

She did wish Edith hadn't arranged for Angie Wilson to help on this project. She tried to tell herself it was because they had nothing in common, but truthfully? She was simply jealous.

She couldn't stand the thought of Angie and Jon together, even though planting that hateful image in the forefront of her mind had made it easier to resist the temptation to dally in the rose arbour with him.

Fuming silently, Jon watched Megan walk swiftly across the lawn.

She'd done it to him again! How was it that *she* was always the self-possessed one when they met?

Obviously, she didn't feel a reciprocal flare of the desire he felt for her, making him tongue-tied in her presence. And who was Bob? His mind latched onto the unknown quantity in the equation. Jon hadn't met any Bob as far as he could recall.

Angie's answers to his carefully put casual questions that evening made him glad for another reason he hadn't offered Megan a ride. He would have been right out of line.

No wonder she had no time for him. Of course, she'd never be interested in *him*.

"Bob Whitman recently took over the butcher shop from his father," Angie had informed him. "He's been working in Tamworth for years. Now he's back in Oxley Crossing and rumour has it that he and Megan Patterson are about to announce their engagement."

Jon refused to identify the cold churning in his stomach as jealousy. He grew angry with himself when his thoughts turned insistently to the woman he now knew he had no right to be thinking of at all.

~~~~~

That bloody pompous ass, Bob Whitman, wasn't anywhere near good enough for a woman as special as Megan Patterson.

Jon knew it wasn't any business of his, but the more he saw of Megan the more he liked her. Respected her too. She wasn't classically beautiful, but she had an understated attractiveness that came from the heart and grew on a man. She was an intelligent woman, with a generous, caring nature.

In his opinion, Bob was an opinionated stuffed shirt who gave every appearance of being more interested in Megan's material assets than her personal ones; an assessment that made him angry on her behalf. Jon was positive Megan wouldn't find the happiness she deserved, married to a man like Whitman.

Someone should warn her. Not him though. It wasn't his place to look out for Megan Patterson. A dark scowl settled on his face as he stoically ignored a sneaking desire to supplant Bob in Megan's affections. He wasn't in the market for a relationship, he reminded himself yet again. He ought to be glad Megan was tied up with Bob, making her unavailable to himself. *'Only I'm not glad at all,'* he thought, savagely kicking at an inoffensive clump of grass.

Later, wielding his paintbrush with more vigour than expertise, Jonathon Armitage muttered dark curses on the conniving duplicity of women.

Anger vied with sheer bloody-minded misery for dominance. So black was his mood, so ferocious his scowl, that when Alan's two young daughters, Melanie and Jocelyn, came over to chat, they'd taken one look at him, then headed off elsewhere. Fast.

That was another hurt on top of all the rest.

It was easier to be natural around them. Only adults needed to be guarded against.

'That damned Angie,' Jon cursed silently again. *'It's all her fault.'*

Of course, he'd been feeling sour already thinking about Megan and Bob, but as soon as they arrived to find Alan and his kids waiting, Angie had hung all over *him*, coming on strong and clinging like a leech when he'd attempted to prise himself loose.

Now Alan had turned surly and wasn't talking to him, and Megan had got all snooty and stared down her nose at him. Bob, sufficiently full of himself to be oblivious to the undercurrents, was the only one he was still on speaking terms with. And he had absolutely nothing he cared to say to Bob.

To top it all off he'd gone and scared the kids. *'Damn it all to hell!'*

Continuing to utter dark imprecations under his breath, Jon slapped the paint on wildly, managing to thoroughly splatter himself in the process. This was absolutely the last do-gooder project he'd let anyone talk him into.

Serve them all right if he climbed on his Harley tonight and just kept going. They probably wouldn't even notice he was gone.

'Not that I care,' he grumbled to himself. *'I don't owe any of them a damned thing!'*

By the lunch break he'd talked himself out of the worst of the anger roiling inside him. Now he was just plain miserable.

There were two places left at the table; beside Bob who was sitting next to Megan, or across from her next to Angie.

Blackly ignoring Angie's invitation to occupy the seat she'd saved for him, Jon defiantly plonked himself down next to Bob, and proceeded to ignore the lot of them. They ignored him right back, except for Melanie and Jocelyn whose whispers and giggles at last succeeded in penetrating his foul mood.

Turning steely eyes on them across the table to discover them staring curiously back at him, Jon felt his mood lighten a little, and winked at them.

No further encouragement was needed. Swamping him with pent-up questions about the Harley, they proceeded to tell him about their own bikes. Their grandfather had given each of them a Peewee 50 for Christmas. They loved motorbikes, they confided.

"When we grow up a bit more, Daddy's going to let us ride in the junior motocross competitions," Melanie informed him with a defiant, sidelong glance at her father, then brought Jon up to date on the local junior dirt bike scene.

Cuppa over, the girls followed Jon back to his paint job, and kept on talking nineteen to the dozen, telling him more than he would ever want to know about the farm, their ponies and school.

Another hour saw all the work finished with time over for a swim in the deep pool below the waterfall before going on to 'Morgan's Run', the Morgan family's property, for the promised barbecue. Jon wished he could get out of it, but without transport of his own, he had no option. He'd just have to suffer it.

After splashing about for a while with Melanie and Jocelyn, Jon left them behind in the shallows.

Swimming away from the others to a quiet spot on the far side of the pool, he turned to float on his back, looking up at the sky, imagining cloud monsters; a game his mother had played with him during his childhood.

'I could float like this forever,' he was thinking. *'At peace, with no damned people intruding and causing a ton of trouble.'*

His pleasant, relaxed mood was abruptly shattered when a sneak attack dragged him under. Floundering and spluttering, struggling to find the right way up, he blinked water out of his eyes and looked for the aggressor. Alan!

"What the bloody hell..." he began furiously. Alan cut in sharply.

"Can it. The ducking was payback for your rotten mood. We need to talk, Jon. About Angie. She's my girl, you know. If I thought for one moment you were trying to make out with her, I'd have given you more than a ducking."

Less certainly, he continued. "You're not though, are you? It's all Angie playing games, isn't it? We had a row and now she's using you to make me jealous."

Jon hastened to agree that, yes, it was only Angie's games. Curious, he had to ask, "How serious is it with you two?"

"I mean to marry her, Jon. As soon as possible when my divorce is finalised." Alan grinned at Jon's raised brow, and explained further as they followed they rest of the party out of the water.

"Janice, my ex, was a city girl I met at university. Getting married was a big mistake for both of us, but Melanie was on the way." He shrugged, dismissing his memories.

"We tried to make a go of it. Trouble was, Jan always hated the bush, and my livelihood is out here. She walked out two years ago, then earlier this year Angie blew into town."

He fixed his eyes on Jon, silently impressing on him the importance of these revelations. "This time it's the real thing for me, Jon. Just so you know. Angie's spoken for."

Alan grinned again and this time Jon returned the grin, relieved to know his conscience was clear.

Relieved, too, to be back on friendly terms with this man he was fast coming to look on as a friend.

He didn't have so many friends he could afford to lose one. Oxley Crossing was bad enough as it was.

Without friends like Alan it would be impossible.

~~~~~

The barbecue proved a success all round. Andrew and Barbara Morgan, Alan's parents, had made everyone welcome, and Angie, with a whispered apology to Jon, decided instead to practice her wiles on Bob. Flattered by her attention, he played along quite happily, much to Jon's surprise and disgust.

If a girl of Megan's calibre was in love with *him* he wouldn't waste his time flirting with the likes of Angie. Was Megan so sure of her man she could calmly sit there and watch him making up to another woman?

Or was Angie wrong, and there was nothing between the two of them at all?

Jon's heart beat a little faster. He wished he knew for sure, one way or the other.

Then cursed himself for letting it matter to him.

Ready to leave, Megan asked Bob for his car keys.

"I'll drive home if you like, Bob," she offered, to be met with a truculent refusal.

Bob wasn't drunk, but he had had a few beers more than she liked in a driver, making her offer a sensible one. On the point of intervening when it seemed an argument might develop, Jon was forestalled by Angie's practised defusing of the situation.

"Of course, you're not drunk, Bob. Nobody thinks you are," she said. "We all know you're perfectly capable of delivering us home safely. Only you know, the word's out that the Highway Patrol have their breathalyser unit working out here this weekend. It's not worth risking your licence over. Here Megan."

She deftly twitched the keys out of Bob's hand and tossed them to the other woman.

"You drive, and I'll sit up front with you. The boys can hold hands in the back."

Knowing Megan to be a good driver, Bob accepted defeat at Angie's hands gracefully, settling into the back seat to doze off.

The trip home proved quite amicable, Jon amused by the budding friendship between the two women in the front seat who had had so little to say to each other on the way out that afternoon.

~~~~~

"I like Megan"' Angie confided to him later, as they entered the side door of the hotel together.

"I didn't think I would. We haven't had much to do with each other before, and I'd written her off as a bit snobbish. Now I've had a chance to get to know her, I can see she's only shy."

Laughing, she added, "You know Jon, Megan said earlier that she envied me. Me! I can't imagine why; she's got it all. Well educated, lots of friends, even her own business. She doesn't know how lucky she is."

~~~~~

'After its disastrous beginning, the day turned out quite well,' Megan thought.

At first, she'd felt sick with disappointment when Jon had been in such a terrible mood. It was awful of her, she knew, only she was really glad it had been Angie, hanging all over him in that embarrassing way of hers, who'd caused it.

She'd felt like murdering them both, until she'd realised Jon was furious with the other girl, disliking the way she clung to him. After that, Megan's own mood had lightened considerably.

'I could have clawed her eyes out though,' Megan thought, ashamed of her jealousy. A pity really, that Angie was like that, unable to leave the men alone. She'd even flirted with Bob.

Not that Megan had minded. It had even been quite liberating, discovering how little she actually felt for Bob; how easily she could cut the ties between them; how little guilt she'd felt in doing so when they were alone later in the evening.

At least now she knew, with absolute certainty, that she would never marry Bob Whitman; an idea she had been toying with before Jon arrived.

But how could she, when he meant so very little to her? Angie had done her a favour there, opening her eyes to the truth.

While she and Angie had been helping Barbara in the kitchen, out of reach of the men, the three of them had got along well, Angie showing herself to be more intelligent and likeable than Megan had previously imagined her to be.

'*She's a rather interesting woman,*' Megan conceded. '*I liked her quite a lot. Perhaps we could even become friends.*' She had lots of friends in The Crossing, but wasn't particularly close to any of them these days, what with most of them being married and her time taken up first with her mother, then establishing her business.

She missed having a special friend to spend girl-time with. Geni was always on the other end of the phone, but it simply wasn't the same. Could Angie Wilson fill the gap?

She shied away from the demeaning idea that friendship with Angie would give her an impeccable reason to invade Jon's lair at the hotel. Although the possibility of getting to know him better held tremendous appeal.

Thinking of Jon again.

She did it far too often, Megan knew, only she didn't seem able to help it. Continuing to think of him, against all her advice to herself, she considered his interaction with Melanie and Jocelyn.

Obviously, he had a soft spot for young children.

Megan filed that important snippet of information away with all the other facts she was gleaning about Jonathon Armitage.

Realising she was still thinking about him, she resolutely rolled over, seeking oblivion in sleep.

6

The following week was busy, busy, busy for Megan. With the new bank's opening day almost upon them, there were numerous last-minute details to attend to.

As committee chairperson, she was hostess for the day, tasked with introducing the bank officials and staff to the people of Oxley Crossing. It had also fallen to Megan to organise the catering and media coverage for the event.

As if all that wasn't enough, her father, released from hospital on Monday, had moved into her downstairs guest room. No stairs, by doctor's orders, meant he wouldn't be returning to his own home above the garage for some time yet. He insisted on helping out where he could, refusing to be fussed over, but was too weak still to do much.

Megan caught only fleeting glimpses of Jonathon Armitage, tiny high points in her busy days as she rushed from one task to the next.

Thursday, deliberately timed to coincide with Oxley Crossing's other big event, the Tidy Towns judging, was opening day.

At eight o'clock Thursday morning, willing volunteers, most with a vested interest, materialised to deck the old bank, resplendent in its fresh new colours of maroon and gold, with bunting and balloons. At nine-thirty on the dot the doors were flung open by the manager to welcome the official party.

Megan made her introductory speech then handed over to Bill Whitman, Bob's father, in his capacity as Council President, to make the obligatory opening speech and cut the ribbon.

Cameras flashing, local reporters, both print and television, recorded the event for posterity, while their regional radio station was broadcasting live, interviewing anyone who could be cornered for a few quick words.

Champagne corks popped amid a flurry of congratulations and best wishes. Elizabeth Tan, employed as caterer for the big event, served canapes and champagne to all who walked through the door.

And everyone, without exception, landed congratulatory kisses on Megan's flushed cheeks.

'*Nothing ventured, nothing gained,*' Jon speculated, indulging himself by joining in with all the others to make the most of this innocuous opportunity. It was a pity there were too many people around to do the job properly.

One little social kiss, with that warm tingly surge of energy to boost its impact, had only served to whet his appetite for more. A lot more.

Perhaps it was just as well they were in the middle of a public gathering.

'Damn Bob Whitman,' Jon thought, remembering Megan's interest in the man. It was time to disappear before he did something silly, making a complete fool of himself. Pausing only long enough to say hello to Angie and Alan who had just entered, together he noted wryly, Jon downed the last of his champagne and took himself off to where his own work awaited him next door.

~~~~~

Too exhausted to cook dinner at the end of what had to have been one of the busiest days of her life, Megan acquiesced gratefully when her father announced he had booked a table down at The Victoria.

"I'm taking you out to celebrate, Meggie" he told her. "You've earned it. Upstairs with you now. You've time for a nice, relaxing soak in the tub before you put on one of those pretty dresses of yours."

Pride mingled with concern in the fond look Mike Patterson sent after his daughter as she hurried up the stairs. Here she was, his lovely clever Meggie. Almost thirty, and still not married. What was wrong with young men these days he fretted? Couldn't they see past flashy figures and hair?

It probably wasn't their fault though, Mike concluded glumly; Megan was just like her mother.

Until the right man came along she wasn't the woman to take much of an interest in any of the others; and sensing it, they left her alone.

He hoped Edith was right with this crazy idea of hers.

He liked the young fellow well enough, but wasn't convinced yet that Jonathon Armitage was the one for his Meggie. Well, time would tell. He'd wait and see.

And keep his fingers crossed.

~~~~~

Megan was starving. There had been no time for lunch and she'd been too excited to eat a proper breakfast. If it hadn't been for Elizabeth pressing little titbits on her from time to time, she doubted she would have eaten anything at all today.

As soon as the official contingent concluded their duties, local residents had poured into the bank to open accounts. All, it seemed, intent on demonstrating their support for *their* bank, as well as being able to boast of being first day customers.

It had been a magnificent opening day's trading, auguring well for the future.

The crush had almost overwhelmed the small staff, who'd roped Megan in to marshal the crowd into waiting patiently in orderly lines.

Meeting Jonathon Armitage at the entrance to the dining room, Mike, to Megan's delight, promptly included him in the celebratory meal, refusing to take no for an answer. Just as they were getting settled, Edith bustled in, full of her own busy day escorting the Tidy Towns judges.

"Today went very well. Most impressed, they were, you know," she assured them, "and very interested in the town's revival epitomised by the bank opening today."

Edith's smile could have lit up the whole room.

"That was a brilliant strategy of yours Meggie. I've heard all about how well the opening went, my girl. Congratulations."

She kissed Megan soundly, then Mike and Jon as well for good measure, sitting down at last in the chair Mike had patiently been holding ready for her.

Edith, unlike Jon, was a guest by prior invitation, Megan realised, amused by Edith's lack of surprise at Jon's presence. She obviously approved of him. Was she still intent on 'saving' him?

Little did she know Mike and Edith were scheming, not only to persuade Jon to change his ways and settle down in Oxley Crossing, but also to throw him into contact with herself, with matchmaking in mind. Eagle-eyed Edith had observed how Megan looked at Jon with an expression in her eyes she had for no-one else.

And Edith was convinced it wasn't by any means a one-way attraction. She had always pooh-poohed the rumours about Bob Whitman, maintaining that when it came down to it, Megan would never marry Bob because she wasn't in love with him.

Now she was busily contriving ways and means to bring about a match with Jonathon Armitage, undaunted by her quarry's elusiveness.

Towards the end of the meal, the conversation turned to the dance on Saturday night.

A regular monthly event, the highly successful charity fund-raisers were an important feature on the Oxley Crossing social calendar.

Employing her usual irresistible technique, Edith wrung a promise from Jon to attend, imperiously claiming him as her partner for the first dance.

"And don't be late, young man," she admonished him playfully. "I object to being kept waiting."

Soon after, the little party broke up. Although it was still early, Mike's fragile strength was flagging and Megan was having trouble stifling her yawns. She longed for her bed and a good night's sleep.

~~~~~

"Thanks Dad. You know I love you lots, don't you?" Megan hugged her father affectionately as she parted from him outside his bedroom. Chuckling contentedly to himself, Mike hugged her back. He knew his daughter loved him. He loved her too, and no father could be prouder of his offspring than he was of his Meggie.

Dozing off to sleep that night, Megan reflected on her day, not surprised that it was Jonathon Armitage's contribution which lingered in her mind.

Smiling sleepily, she mused on how much she had enjoyed his presence at dinner. Just for once he'd been in a mellow, approachable mood, meeting her eyes across the table with a smile. No scowls or icy glares tonight.

He was really very good company when he relaxed, allowing others to get close. It was a long time since she'd enjoyed the company of a well-informed man, whose wide-ranging conversation was free of the small-town bias she found so frustrating in some of the locals, much as she liked them.

'He's suffered though,' she thought, 'to make him so untrusting. I wonder what it was.' Maybe Edith knew what she was about, after all, she thought drowsily. However, her Jonathon Armitage was still very much a mystery man.

Almost her last thought before sleep claimed her, Megan remembered how Jon had kissed her that morning; along with so many others.

It was the fleeting touch of Jon's lips on her cheek that had buoyed her up all day, though. The pity was, it had been too public. Too impersonal and too quickly over to even qualify as a proper kiss.

Reliving it yet again as she drifted into sleep, Megan recalled the lovely heart-warming surge of energy that accompanied it.

"That's what it is," she murmured, "it's energy. Life energy. Whenever I touch him, the energy of Jon's life-force flows into me. No wonder he makes me feel so alive.'

SAVING JONATHON ARMITAGE

7

Wincing as he flexed muscles cramped from working on the underbelly of a car, Jon stretched the kinks out as he rose to his feet. Frowning irritably, he complained to himself.

'The damned woman's still here. What could possibly take so long on a Saturday morning? Hasn't she got better things to do with her time?' He'd been able to hear Megan's cheerful voice off and on all morning, chatting to Jack O'Hara in the office.

After letting down his guard Thursday night he was now in full retreat, attempting to restore his protective camouflage of cold indifference. Trying hard to convince himself the indifference was genuine.

Painfully bitter experience had seared into his psyche the folly of trusting his happiness to others. Especially when those others were women.

It was better to hold himself aloof.

Safer.

'And,' he reminded himself grimly, *'there are worse fates than being alone.'*

If only he could figure out a way to distance himself from that infuriatingly desirable Megan Patterson, with her damnably tempting friendliness!

Unfortunately, the more he tried to stay away from her, the more he wanted to get close. Needed to get close? His mind shut down abruptly when faced with that scary thought, refusing to contemplate it for even a moment.

His face twisted into a savage grimace as a brief peal of laughter announcing Megan's continued presence assaulted his ears.

He was about to slide back under the car on the creeper and finish the job so he could make his escape, when the opening of the workshop door halted him.

'What now!' Jon seethed, lips tightening.

And then in bustled his Nemesis. Megan, as usual, was all happy smiles, at the same time both repelling and attracting Jon; heightening his already dangerously confused and frustrated mood.

In anticipation of the treat she'd been promising herself all morning – sharing a precious few minutes alone with Jonathon Armitage, - Megan chose to ignore his all too familiar scowl.

A steaming mug in each hand, she greeted him blithely.

"Morning Jon. I've just finished balancing the books and Jack's made coffee."

She held up two mugs of steaming coffee. "Thought you could probably do with one too, by now."

The fragrant aroma of freshly brewed coffee blended harmoniously with the harsher smell of engine oil that, over long years, had impregnated the very walls of the workshop.

It created a familiar combination of odours that had always spelt the warmth and security of her father to Megan. Her trusting smile invited Jon to share her innocent pleasure in the moment.

Hot desire flooded through Jon at the mere sight of Megan Patterson standing there smiling naively up at him. He wanted her, in the worst conceivable way. Temptation grew, overwhelming rational thought until sensible resistance became too much for him. He couldn't take Megan's unknowing torment a moment longer.

Something snapped, breaking free deep inside him.

Something he'd been keeping on a tight leash ever since he'd met Megan Patterson. Until now. When he lost his grip.

Her smile faltering as Jon's scowl grew even blacker, his eyes glittering hectically through narrowed slits, Megan mutely thrust one of the steaming mugs into his hand.

'What's eating him?' she wondered. *'He was so nice Thursday night and now it seems he's back to hating the entire world and everyone in it worse than ever. Especially me, it seems. What have I done?'*

Puzzled, but refusing to be daunted by Jon's inexplicable black mood, Megan stood, transfixed by the unblinking glare he'd turned on her, a presentiment of danger waking too late.

Without breaking eye contact, Jon slowly put down his untouched coffee and reached out, taking Megan's from her unresisting hand to put it, with deliberate care, beside his own on the bench.

Still without a word, still compelling her eyes with his own, Jon stepped in close.

Real close.

Too close.

His hands gripped her shoulders, hauling her up against the hard angles of his body.

Mouth suddenly dry, Megan felt her heartbeat accelerate wildly. Hardly daring to breathe, she watched Jon, mesmerised by the danger she read in storm-darkened grey eyes.

Until she detected a minuscule softening in his steely expression. Enough to set her heart singing, rising excitement banishing her momentary fear.

Was Jonathon Armitage about to kiss her? It seemed he was. All thought of danger vanished leaving eager anticipation in its wake.

A flame of pure joy flared in Megan's heart as Jon's lips lowered towards hers.

Instantly her own parted, inviting him in. Milliseconds later her lips were crushed in a heady assault.

The pleasant tingling electricity she had grown accustomed to exploded into a lightning bolt, flashing and thundering across her nerve ends, ripping apart her carefully nurtured caution and exposing within her a previously undetected well of sensuality.

Megan almost cried out in wonder when Jon's tongue began stroking the sensitive inner lining of her mouth while his hands ran deliciously down her back to her hips, pulling her up hard against his already rampant erection.

Megan leaned in closer, hands reaching up to clasp hungrily round his neck. *'Heaven!'* Megan exulted silently. *'I'm in heaven.'* Then she was beyond further thought. Lost. Revelling in the searing passion of their deepening kiss.

Lips fused and tongues danced a tango for two as Jon sank into the intoxicating sweetness that was Megan's mouth. A sweetness rendered all the more seductive by his prior self-denial. His earlier resolve was swept away on a tidal wave of desire that would no longer be denied; and he succumbed. In spite of his determination not to get involved.

Never before had Megan been so thoroughly kissed; and never before had she kissed back so enthusiastically.

A whirling maelstrom of hot, melting sensation swept her along on its crest. Jon's urgently roving hands were everywhere, caressing and kneading her soft flesh, demanding she respond. And she did, threading urgent fingers through his hair and pressing her hips sinuously against his delectably hard body as if seeking to meld the two of them into one fiery being.

When her fingers caressed his throat where she felt his blood pumping as fast and furiously as her own she revelled in the discovery and made tacit demands of her own. *'More! More!'* She couldn't get enough of this man's passion.

Couldn't give him enough of her own.

When Jon's searching fingers demanded ever greater intimacies, deftly slipping buttons from their rightful places, Megan didn't draw back as she had always done with other men. Even though she vaguely felt she should.

But this was Jon. Her Jon. And Megan could deny him nothing. Would deny him nothing. Instead, she urged him on, greedily meeting his demands and answering them with urgent demands of her own. Suddenly insatiable, she silently demanded more.

Other kisses had been enjoyable, but Jonathon's kiss way exceeded enjoyable. Megan revelled in his mastery over her, driven to eager compliance in his possession of her, knowing instinctively that she possessed him equally; thrilled at her own burgeoning feminine power.

Totally oblivious of their surroundings, responding mindlessly to their need for each other, neither Megan nor Jon heard the door open quietly to admit Mike.

Half a glance was sufficient to convince Mike Patterson he'd better get himself out of there.

Fast.

Before either of them became aware of his presence.

The last thing he wanted to do was embarrass his little girl. She was all grown up now and he trusted her. At least he had until a minute ago. Now he wasn't so sure.

As for that Jonathon Armitage...

Well! He couldn't decide whether to be glad someone finally appreciated his daughter or explode into paternal outrage.

But Megan would hate that, so he took a couple of deep breaths and reigned in the anger as he backed out the door.

Mike pulled the door almost closed behind him.

"Jon? You still around, Jon?" he called out while looking around for something noisy to drop on the floor. He followed up by swearing over-loudly at the resulting clatter. Taking the time to clear up the mess first, he re-entered the workshop, calling out again he pushed the door open.

Daring to look, he spotted Jon sliding under a car and the back-door swinging closed as Megan made a hasty escape. Permitting himself a sly grin at the sight of two rapidly cooling coffees abandoned on the workbench, Mike called out innocently.

"There you are. Letter for you, Jon. I remembered I didn't clear the post box yesterday. There was this one for you mixed in with mine." Mike handed the letter to the younger man as he slid out again from under the car and stood up; a bit flushed, Mike observed. Jon glanced distractedly at the letter in his hand without actually seeing it.

"Thanks Mike. I've got to get this job finished," he muttered, and tossed the letter carelessly onto the bench as he dived back under cover.

~~~~~

Mike kept a cheerfully observant eye on his daughter for the rest of the morning, tickled pink at what he was seeing. Megan was blooming, humming softly while she tidied up around the house; losing herself from time to time in blissful daydreams.

'*Maybe Eddie is right,*' Mike thought. '*Won't she be over the moon when I tell her!*'

~~~~~

'*It really happened,*' Megan thought jubilantly. It hadn't been her imagination. She hadn't been the only one who had lost control either. Jon's passion had been every bit as wildly abandoned as her own. There'd been none of his customary aloofness during those heady minutes in the garage. She wasn't terribly experienced with men, although she'd kissed quite a satisfying number of frogs in her fruitless search for a prince. However, it didn't take any experience at all to recognise that Jon's intense response had been driven by more than casual lust.

Their encounter had been too primal, too genuine. Too lacking in calculation. Besides, men didn't lust after ordinary girls like her, did they? Not to the point of losing control. Did that mean it was love?

"Does he love me as much as I love him?" she asked herself dreamily.

Realising what she had just said, she hugged herself rapturously, whispering, "I'm in love! I'm in love with Jonathon Armitage! No wonder I can't stop thinking about him all the time." A gurgle of joyous laughter bubbled from between her lips. What a pity her father had interrupted at exactly that moment, before Jon had time to declare himself.

Giggling to herself, Megan recalled the shock on Jon's face when her father's voice, followed by the bang and clatter of dislodged cans, had sent them springing apart.

He'd moved like greased lightning, urging her towards the back door before ducking for cover himself.

Catching a horrified glimpse of her own disordered clothing – when had those buttons come undone? - she had raced away with equal speed. It would never do to let her father see her in such a disordered state.

To him she was still his little girl, and he would have been hurt and offended by her wantonness.

Blushing at the memory, Megan changed her mind, glad her father hadn't entered a few moments later. He might have had a relapse if he had. Neither she nor Jon had been in the mood to stop.

Even now her body burned with frustrated longing just thinking of the way Jon had been touching and kissing her. Fiercely pulling her to him while he devoured her with his kisses.

If this was the difference love made, no wonder she'd always been so depressingly indifferent to other men's kisses.

Bubbling with expectation, Megan set about fixing lunch. Sufficient for three, she decided, tossing a generous salad made from her own home-grown vegetables. Surely Jon would want to see her again when he finished work, then she would casually invite him to join them. Daydreaming with a soppy smile on her lips, she settled down to wait for her lover.

Until Mike's plaintively voiced enquiry some time later.

"Any chance of some lunch sometime soon, Meggie love, or are we holding a rehearsal for the Forty Hour Famine?"

Unable then to keep her father waiting any longer, Megan served the meal. Minus her desired guest.

Disappointed by Jon's non-appearance, she comforted herself by recalling that really, in her rush to escape, she hadn't had time to invite Jon to lunch. Perhaps he was unsure of his reception.

Especially since she didn't get a chance to tell him of her love, Megan rationalised.

Her newly discovered love leaving her too shy to openly seek him out, she devised an alternative strategy that would make it easy for Jon to approach *her*. Wearing her prettiest sun-dress, she took a rug, cushion and book to spend the afternoon reading in the park opposite the hotel.

Not that she did very much reading, being too busy keeping a close watch on the comings and goings opposite, hoping Jon would see her there and come over to join her.

Thoughtfully, she arranged herself in an artfully attractive pose. To no avail. Waiting till nearly four o'clock, Megan finally abandoned her post. He must have gone out, she thought sadly, never once considering Jon mightn't be as eager to continue where he'd left off as herself.

Remembering hopefully that tonight was dance night, and she knew for certain Jon was planning to attend - he'd promised Edith the first dance, hadn't he - she hurried home. This time she would be pampering and preening herself for Jonathon Armitage. Tonight, she'd go all out to look her very best for him.

That evening, wearing a new taffeta party dress in her favourite blue, an impulse buy she'd been saving for a special occasion, Megan had love in her heart and a spring in her step when she walked round the block to the hall with her father.

'Let it be Jonathon Armitage who walks me home tonight,' she prayed.

~~~~~

Jon's mind was in turmoil. Castigating himself for his careless stupidity, he wondered how he could have let his guard down so far as to do the very thing he'd sworn not to. What if Mike had caught them? If he had, there would undoubtedly have been an embarrassing scene. Maybe worse. The old man was generally pretty easy going, but Megan was his darling.

'I didn't mean to kiss her,' he excused himself morosely, *'only she was too tempting to resist any longer.'*

Remembering how desire had roared through him like a firestorm at the first taste of Megan's sweetness, erasing everything from his mind but his own raging need, he drove his hands through his hair in frustration.

As if that justified his breaking his own cardinal rule on non-involvement, he sneered at himself. What if he'd inadvertently awakened in Megan expectations he couldn't meet?

He had nothing to offer a girl who was so obviously made for permanency, while he was strictly temporary.

Jon's anger spread to include Megan. She'd brought it on herself, intruding in his domain where she wasn't wanted. And what about Bob?

Megan's behaviour was hardly that of a loyal fiancée. Their encounter hadn't been one-way by any means. Jon felt himself growing hot and hard remembering how they had both been equally carried away.

If Mike hadn't interrupted them, he was afraid he'd have taken her without another thought. Right there in the dirt and grease on the workshop floor. Jon shuddered, but whether in frustration or self-disgust he didn't know. And preferred not to.

It was all Megan's fault.

If he could only convince himself of that, maybe he could assuage his guilt. Determined, he tried to ignore the unwelcome little voice in the back of his mind that whispered Megan had no business marrying Bob, or anyone else, when she could kiss *him* as she had that morning.

It was time to bail out before he got in any deeper.Time to load up the saddlebags, wheel out the Harley and hit the road.

On Monday, he'd tell Mike to find someone else; then he'd be out of here.

~~~~~

During the afternoon, he saw Megan in the park.

Brooding, he battled against his instinct to go to her. Desire warred with his newly reiterated resolve to keep his distance, but this time he held firm. Virtuously, he convinced himself disappearing from her life was the best thing he could do for Megan.

Although this time he clung firmly to his decision to avoid temptation, he couldn't resist indulging himself by watching her from a safe distance.

'One day she'll thank me,' he assured himself, staunchly ignoring the bleakness that flooded through him at the thought of never seeing Megan Patterson again.

'*Damn!*' Tonight was dance night. Jon seriously considered reneging on his promise to attend. He would have, except that if he did, he wouldn't put it past Edith Turner to come after him. Could he avoid Megan at the dance? No way was he going to risk going anywhere near her again.

Just the thought of dancing with Megan, holding her close in his arms, made him go hot and cold all over. Looking wildly about him, desperately searching for some means of escape, his eye caught a flash of red hair.

Angie.

Jon recalled that Marge had given her the night off to go to the dance. Angie had used him for her own purposes more than once. Tonight, Jon would return the favour. He needed a shield against temptation, and Angie Wilson would do just fine.

Acting on impulse, he went after her, inviting her to walk round to the hall with him.

~~~~~

From the centre of the group of friends crowding around herself and Mike, Megan watched Jon enter with his arm draped round Angie's shoulders, his head bent attentively to catch what she was saying; and her blood ran cold.

'*They both live at the hotel,*' she told herself, clutching at straws, '*so it's only natural they would walk round together.*'

She tried in vain to ignore the intimacy of Jon's arm holding Angie so closely against his side.

As soon as he could free himself, surely Jon would come to her, and ask her to dance.

She just needed to be a little bit patient, Megan decided. Only it didn't work out that way.

Edith had swooped on him immediately, prying him loose from Angie and whisking him out onto the floor to join the military two-step just beginning. After that, instead of dancing with Megan, Jon had proceeded to stand up with almost every woman present except her. He danced more than once with Angie and stuck like glue to her between dances, laughing and joking with Alan and the other single men swarming round the vivacious redhead like bees round a honey pot.

Megan had managed to catch his eye quite early on, but when she did, he deliberately looked right through her as if she didn't exist, scotching any idea she may have had about following Edith's example and taking the initiative. After that cruel rebuff, Megan concentrated on stifling her heartache. On hiding her pain from prying eyes till she could succumb to it in private.

The Oxley Crossing gossip mill wasn't going to use Megan Patterson for grist.

No way.

She lifted her head proudly, fixing a brave smile to her lips. Even without Jonathon Armitage, Megan didn't lack partners. Dancing every dance, she permitted herself no time to brood over Jon's betrayal.

Except ...

Except that he hadn't actually made any promises. Even though Megan believed in her heart that their wonderful kiss this morning had of itself constituted an unspoken promise.

She smiled and smiled. Smiled till her face hurt, so no-one watching would suspect that beneath her bright smile, her heart was breaking.

The only good thing to come of her night out occurred when Bob White quietly apologised, asking if they could go back to being friends, hastily assuring her he quite understood there was no chance they would ever be more than friends and neighbours.

Megan hadn't confided in anybody what had happened when Bob had seen her home after the Morgan's barbecue. Not even her father. Especially not her father, weak as he still was in the aftermath of his heart attack. Scrupulously, she sheltered him from everything which might upset him.

Since Bob had returned to Oxley Crossing on his father's retirement he'd been paying court to her, letting her know he was ready to settle down and had chosen her, Megan Patterson, as a suitable spouse. Although neither was in love with the other, Megan was flattered. Bob was an undemonstrative man whom she'd known since their school days. A man she liked and respected, finding him a pleasant companion, if a slightly pompous one on occasion.

One whose marriage plans she had begun to consider seriously.

She wanted a family, babies, and she had begun to hear a muted ticking emanating from her biological clock. First, though, she needed to find her future babies a father, and Bob Whitman had been the only prospect on her horizon.

He'd come in for coffee with her the night of the barbecue, as he often had.

This time was different, though. This time, spurred to false bravado by the beer he'd consumed, he'd grabbed Megan, catching her unawares when he began kissing her forcefully, refusing to release her when she struggled.

Previously, his kisses had been mild, pleasant, easily ended when she'd had enough of him. This time he'd tightened his grip, pressing himself against her while attempting to overpower her. He was far stronger than Megan, and he'd frightened her.

Fortunately, her determined resistance had pierced his ego and he'd backed off, deflated, accusing her of being a tease and becoming sulky when she protested.

"I'm tired of being fobbed off, Meggie! In this day and age there's no need to wait till after we're married."

"Bob, I know you think you want to marry me," Megan answered, trying to placate him, "and I'm flattered. Really. I've given your offer a great deal of serious thought. But I can't marry you, Bob. I like you, and would have been proud to be your wife, only I've discovered liking isn't enough. I need to be in love with the man I marry."

"What about all the stories you hear of love growing after marriage? You could learn to love me, couldn't you?"

"Oh Bob, I'm sorry. But if you look in your own heart, I'm sure you'll realise you don't really love me either."

Bob knew his feelings for Megan were only lukewarm, but, a possessive man, he'd gotten used to thinking of her as his future wife. His only reply had been an angry glare, before he slammed out the door, its echo reverberating in Megan's ears leaving her shaken and tearful.

She found it was a relief, being on speaking terms again. Oxley Crossing was too small for feuds.

Jon left the dance early, Angie by his side once again.

Shortly after, Megan, close to the limits of her emotional endurance, insisted her father say goodnight to his friends and go home with her. He'd paced himself carefully, only allowing himself one sedate foxtrot with his old friend, Edith, and he rebelled against his daughter's edict.

When Megan begged him not to overreach his strength, it was Edith who supported her. Edith, whose words were heeded.

"Come on now, Mike," Edith jollied him along, "stop behaving like an old fool. It's time to get you home, before we have Doc Rogers over here babbling on about relapses."

To Megan's surprise and relief, Mike stopped protesting and left without any more fuss.

SAVING JONATHON ARMITAGE

8

Alone in her bedroom at last, Megan collapsed onto her bed in a storm of tears. How could she have been so naïve as to imagine Jonathon Armitage returned her love? Their kiss had obviously meant less than nothing to him.

Oh, but it hurt to give her heart for the first time, only to have it cruelly rejected. She thumped her pillow in pain and fury.

Self-pity segued into healthy anger.

"I hate him!"

Megan sobbed, furiously thumping her pillow again for emphasis, wishing it was Jonathon Armitage she was thumping.

"I hate him!" she gasped, working hard to turn words into reality. It was so much easier to believe she hated Angie Wilson. Easier to convince herself the other girl had betrayed their nascent friendship. Megan was glad now she'd been too busy to follow through on her tentative plan to get to know Angie.

There was no room in Megan's heart now for friendship with Angie Wilson.

Not while Jonathon Armitage stood between them.

~~~~~

'God, I feel such a heel,' Jon berated himself. *'Such a low-down rotten excuse for a man.'*

Tonight, he'd done more than merely avoid Megan. Tonight, he'd deliberately set about destroying whatever feelings Megan had for him.

Tonight, he'd panicked.

Meeting her eyes across the hall, he'd seen what he thought might be love light up her face. And he'd panicked. He'd felt the old trap of emotional involvement closing in on him and he'd panicked, reacting more cruelly than necessary to extricate himself.

His escape hadn't been without cost to himself, either.

Repudiating Megan Patterson had been one of the hardest things Jon had ever done.

In the short time he'd known Megan, regardless of his efforts to be impervious to the attraction she held for him, she'd sneaked into his heart. He'd developed a grudging fondness for her and he'd let his guard down, allowing her in.

Now he was paying the price. Now Megan was paying the price. The guilty pain he was suffering on Megan's behalf had catapulted him back to the misery of being rejected by his family nearly ten years earlier. Then, he was the only victim of his misplaced chivalry.

This time Megan, the one he'd tried to protect from the darkness within himself, had been hurt as well. If only he hadn't panicked, he could have got his message across less painfully.

Somehow.

Every time he attempted good, it turned out bad.

Rising with the sun after a night of guilty tossing and turning in fruitless pursuit of sleep, Jon took off on the Harley, attempting to out-ride his bitterness and self-loathing. His most cowardly instincts urged him to ride on, to keep on going and never turn back. Conscience prohibited such an easy escape. His conscience, and a nebulous something he shied away from acknowledging.

Turning back at last, he persuaded himself it was only because he'd given his word.

He simply couldn't leave Old Man Patterson in the lurch. What if he did, and it led to another heart attack?

If Mike did have a relapse, Jon vowed it wasn't going to be down to him. But what to do about Megan?

He would simply have to try harder to avoid crossing her trail. He would have to keep himself strictly to himself. She'd probably make it easy for him anyway.

After his brutal snub, Megan was hardly likely to want to be pals any longer, if she ever had.

For the few days it would take to work out his notice, he'd cope. He'd have to. On that dismal thought, Jon turned the Harley back towards Oxley Crossing, already counting the days till he could ride off and never turn back.

~~~~~

Awake early, swollen-eyed and leaden-hearted, Megan heard the distant burble of the Harley leaving town at dawn.

"So the rat's running, is he?" she muttered. "He'd better. I'll kill him if I ever see him again." No she wouldn't. Fresh tears oozed weakly from puffy, reddened eyes to trail down pallid cheeks. Anger, even though righteous, had been beyond her power to maintain. He was thoroughly unworthy, but she still loved the dratted man. If Jonathon Armitage came to her, sincerely begging her forgiveness, Megan knew in her heart she'd grant it in an instant.

Hating herself for such weakness, she stumbled into the shower. Laughing wildly, she recalled the song from 'South Pacific' and in a pathetic attempt at humour, she croaked a few bars, lathering up her hair to match her actions to the words. Abandoning the song as a bad idea, she gave herself a much needed pep-talk instead.

"I might not be able to wash that man right out of my hair, but I won't let him destroy me. I'm not some fragile Victorian damsel about to go into a decline over unrequited love. No more tears now, girl. Life goes on, and you need to go out there and live it. Broken hearts are only painful, not fatal, so pull yourself together Megsie. Unlike some people, you don't have the option of jumping on your bike and running away."

A mug of extra-strong coffee and a half hour in the serenity of her garden went a long way to restoring outward normality. Still cringing inwardly at the effort required to face even her beloved father, Megan threw together a lunch of crackers, fruit and juice.

Checking hurriedly on Mike, she grabbed her daypack and was off. A long solitary hike was the medicine she prescribed for her malady.

If she walked far enough, she might tire herself out enough to sleep tonight.

~~~~~

Barely had Megan left the house than Mike, deeply troubled, went rushing out in search of his fellow conspirator.

After such a promising beginning, their grand matchmaking scheme appeared to have come crashing down around their ears.

His daughter was all the family he had, and Mike wanted above all else, for Megan to be happy. The quick glimpse he'd had of her strained white face, red-rimmed eyes and painful attempt at a smile which turned out more of a grimace, had shocked and upset him.

Bursting through the open back door into Edith's kitchen, he began speaking without preamble.

"Eddie, we've got problems. It's all falling apart on us. You've got to think of something, Eddie. Fast!"

Calmly soothing Mike's badly ruffled feathers and putting a cup of tea and a plate of toast in front of him, Edith sat down. Over breakfast she proceeded to get to the bottom of the problem. They had both observed, unhappily, how Jon had steered clear of Megan at the dance, but now when Mike told Eddie about the interrupted kiss, she briefly doubted her own wisdom.

"... kissing like there was no tomorrow, Eddie,' Mike told her, and elaborated on Megan's euphoria afterwards that contrasted so starkly with her tear-sodden morning face.

"Drat that boy! I wish I could shake some sense into him. Hurting our Meggie like that!" Edith sipped her tea, lost in thought. Mike munched toast, calm again and totally confident of his friend's ability to come up with a satisfactory solution.

"You know Mike, Jon must have been badly hurt sometime in his past, to behave like that. He's very attracted to our Meggie all right. More than he knows, I think. I believe he's running scared."

"Time!" she said, slapping her hand on the table, making Mike jump. "Time, Mike. We need to pin him down here in The Crossing long enough to tear down his defences and teach him to believe in himself and trust others. It's time he stopped playing the lone wolf.' She slapped the table again."

"Until he faces up to his past, Mike, Jon won't be free to return Meggie's love."

Neither of them, confident Megan's heart wasn't involved, had ever given much credence to the rumours about Bob White. Now, firmly convinced Jonathon Armitage was the man she'd given her heart to, they put their heads together to come up with a plan to buy the time Edith swore they needed.

Always provided Jon didn't up and leave immediately as Mike half feared he might.

"No, no, Jon won't do that, Mike. He's got a good heart and good manners," Edith reassured him with a pat on his shoulder as she cleared the dishes.

"Someone brought him up right. I'm sure he won't abandon you without notice. Remember now, your job is to keep him here in The Crossing as long as possible. Wring a promise out of him, Mike. Any way you can. I'm sure he'd hesitate to break a formal promise. Buy us time, and we'll take it from there."

Getting up, Mike crossed to where Edith stood at the sink and hugged her.

"You're a good woman Eddie Turner, and a good friend. The best. I don't know what I'd do without you." Catching a soft, vulnerable look in her eyes, he bent and kissed her.

A long, lingering kiss.

"I love you, you know Eddie," Mike said quietly. "Since my heart attack, I've had a lot of time to think; to get things straight in my head. That heart attack was a warning, but if I do as Doc says I've got a good few years ahead of me yet. And there's two things I want. I want to see Meggie safely married and happy with a couple of grandkids for me to spoil. And I want you, Eddie. I loved my Jenny, but she's gone, and since then I've grown to love you. Will you marry me and make me a happy man, Eddie?"

"Oh Mike, of course I will." Edith, blushing rosily, kissed him back as enthusiastically as a young girl in love for the first time.

"I love you too, Mike. My Stan's been gone for fifteen years now and lately I've been waiting for you to finish grieving for Jenny. I know she'd be happy for us, Mike. Jenny was too generous a woman to want you to be alone for the rest of your life. Let's not wait too long my dear. We're neither of us youngsters any longer so we should make the most of the time we've got left to us."

Agreeing wholeheartedly, Mike shelved his worries about his daughter and set about exploring his new-found chance at love and happiness with his old friend.

Feeling it would be cruel to flaunt their happiness in the face of Megan's present misery, they decided against making an immediate announcement. Megan was strong. She'd come to terms with this setback before long, then they could share their news with her.

More optimistic, and far happier than when he'd arrived, Mike left Edith's house that afternoon to go home and fix something special for Megan's dinner. She'd told him she intended to follow Morgan's Creek to its junction with the river, then through the gorge and home across country over the hills. A round trip of almost twenty kilometres. She would be tired when she returned, and hopefully in a mood to appreciate a bit of pampering from her old dad. Smiling contentedly, Mike donned an apron and got busy in the kitchen.

~~~~~

The long walk had helped Megan to rationalise events. Still heartsick, but knowing she was strong enough to live with it, she resolved to adopt a brisk attitude and keep as fully occupied as possible.

Work would be her panacea. Her shield. Her salvation.

Undoubtedly, she had blown the whole episode out of proportion. Looking back, she was sure it was mostly her own fault. Jon had most likely only responded to her own desire for him, realising later that because he didn't feel anything special for her, it would be cruel to arouse false hopes.

If he hadn't left town for good, she would distance herself from him for the rest of his stay. A short stay if the gods were kind.

Surely such a new love would die quickly if she denied it nourishment.

That bleakly optimistic resolution gave Megan the strength to get through the next few days, and if her eyes strayed too often across the fence, seeking glimpses of a tall, dark, overalled figure, then she determinedly ignored it.

~~~~~

Jon clung determinedly to his two decisions; to avoid Megan, and to cut his stay in Oxley Crossing short. Accordingly, he went to see Mike as early Monday morning as possible, after he was sure Megan had gone through to her office.

Mindful of Eddie's advice, Mike, who'd seen him crossing the back garden, was ready for him.

He assumed a shaky weakness designed to appeal to any compassionate tendencies there might be in the younger man's nature.

"Mike, I'm handing in my notice. I'd like to be out of here Friday at the latest." The bald statement came out sounding harsher than Jon had intended.

Mike gasped, hand rising protectively to cover his chest.

He groped blindly for a chair and sat down heavily, his breath too rapid to be normal. Jon ran to the sink, fetching him a glass of water.

"I'm sorry, Mike. Are you alright? I didn't mean to shock you."

Shakily accepting the water, Mike weakly gestured for Jon to sit in the chair across from him. Sipping slowly, he played for time and effect, gathering his thoughts before launching into his prepared speech.

"I don't understand, Jon. I believed I could count on you for another month or two at least. I'm sure Meggie told me you'd signed on for three months with an option for longer if I needed you."

Mike allowed a pitiful quaver to enter his voice. By thinking sad thoughts, he even generated a little moisture in the corners of his eyes.

"If you really want to leave, I can't keep you here of course." Wringing his hands, Mike infused his words with sad resignation. "You're a good mechanic, Jon. My customers trust you. I thought you'd settled down in The Crossing for a while, that you were making friends here."

He sneaked a peek through lowered lashes, pleased with the guilt clearly evident on Jon's face.

Maybe Eddie had been right. Maybe Jon wasn't the sort to leave a poor, helpless old bloke in the lurch.

Encouraged, Mike sighed heavily, injecting as much pathos into his performance as he could.

"I'm sorry," Jon repeated, guilt and misery chasing each other across his downcast face.

"I'm sorry too, Jon. It's been a real weight off my mind, being able to rely on you. Replacing you at short notice isn't going to be easy. I might even have to close up permanently, and that would be bad for the town, as well as me."

Mike brushed his hand across his face in a gesture of defeat, sighing again. "I'll draft an ad for the papers; get the wheels in motion," he said, adopting a plaintive tone. He hesitated, fixing pathetic eyes on the younger man.

"I know it's a lot to ask, Jon, but do you think you could hang on a bit longer? Just to give me time to find someone?"

Torn between his compulsion to leave and his inbred dislike of letting down anyone to whom he'd given his word, Jon made the mistake of looking directly into Mike's pleading face.

The old man looked on the point of collapse. Jon knew he'd never be able to live with himself if he caused him to have another, possibly fatal, heart attack. Mike's fragility undermining his resolution, Jon heard himself agreeing to stay.

"Only until you get someone else, though, Mike," he qualified.

"I really do want to get away as soon as possible." Afraid of conceding more, Jon terminated the interview and retreated to work, cursing himself for his weakness.

~~~~~

Waiting to be sure Jon wasn't coming back, Mike discarded his portrayal of a tottering invalid. Around to the library he scooted in triumph, to report to Edith.

"You should have seen me, Eddie. I put on a real Oscar-winning tearjerker of a performance. By the time I finished with him, Jon was falling over himself agreeing to stay until I get a replacement for him. I was good, Eddie. Really good. Perhaps I should take up acting."

Enjoying his preening, Edith rewarded him suitably before bringing him back to earth.

"We have to stall now, Mike. Jon will expect to see your ads in the papers, so they'd better be there. Sit down here and I'll help you. Except for Jon, Meggie got no takers with hers, so I don't expect we need worry too much about other applicants."

They settled for a short, simple advertisement which Edith employed the library computer to dispatch to the regional newspapers.

If anyone did inquire about the job, Mike decided he would put them off. He and Eddie were thinking positively about this.

They wanted Jon, and somehow, by hook or by crook, they would keep him in Oxley Crossing. Time and propinquity should take care of the romantic elements, and if a little extra should be needed, then they were ready, willing and able to give Cupid a helping hand.

Edith, an experienced matchmaker, refused to even consider the possibility of failing the young woman, soon to be her stepdaughter, whom they both loved so dearly.

9

With Megan and Jon plotting divergent courses however, progress was too slow to please the conspirators. Impatient, they decided to give fate a gentle nudge.

Those two stubborn young people were never going to arrive at the happy ever after stage unless someone took the initiative and brought them together.

Without consulting Megan, Mike invited Jack O'Hara, his wife Judy and their daughter Susan who worked part-time in the service station, to a barbecue. Their acceptance confirmed, he tackled Jon. Explaining that he wanted to get all of them together to discuss the future of the business, he made it impossible for Jon to refuse.

Megan was the last one Mike approached. And also the from whom to win her co-operation.

"This is really important to me Meggie," he wheedled.

"You won't have to do a thing, you know, except enjoy yourself with our friends, since Eddie's promised to help with the food. I've got something good to tell you all," he hinted, "and I really need my daughter's support. You wouldn't let me down, would you Meggie?"

Unhappy though she was at the prospect of sharing a table with Jon, Megan gave in gracefully to her father's demands.

~~~~~

Saturday arrived, and with Edith's help, Mike soon had all his guests settled comfortably.

Even Megan and Jon managed to be civil to each other he noted, although each had wasted no time moving apart and falling into conversation with someone else.

Food first, Mike decreed, then they could get down to serious talking. Accordingly, after sending Susan's two young sons off to watch a video he'd hired for them, Mike opened his agenda.

"Doc's told me I have to give up working in the garage," he began. "Too much heavy lifting for the old ticker, I'm afraid. I'm not ready to be put out to pasture yet, though. I've still got a few good years in me, and as long as I take it easy, Doc's agreeable to my doing light work.

"These last couple of weeks I've been having a good think about things, and this is what I've decided." He took a moment to glance around his audience.

Reassured he had everyone's undivided attention, he continued.

"There's no need for me to sell up. That would leave me at a loose end. I don't want to work for someone else, and I don't want to be bothered with starting a completely new business at my age. I'm going to take a man on permanently to run the garage side of things for me. Jon," he turned to the younger man, an earnest expression on his face. "I know you weren't planning on staying permanently, but you're a fine mechanic and a man I know I can trust. I'd like you to reconsider. Don't be in a rush, think it over carefully before you decide. The garage is yours if you want it. You'll have seen for yourself there's enough business to generate a comfortable living."

Taking a sip of his drink while he let that idea sink in, Mike carried on talking.

"Jack and Susan, I hope you two will continue working the pumps for me the way you have been lately. I can't see any reason to make changes there, as long as you're both happy."

The two of them murmured their agreement.

"Now for where I plan to fit in. Before Jenny died, we were making plans to expand the coffee bar in the service station into a take-away cafe. Without Jenny, I lost interest in the project, but now I feel ready to give it a try. I'm not such a bad cook myself, and Judy? How do you feel about helping me out part-time?"

Mike's suggestion generated an excited discussion. Positive ideas flowed freely, and Judy, pleased to be included in the project, readily agreed to join the team.

Jon sat quietly on the sidelines, envious of the easy friendship and trust existing between these people. A friendship and trust they were willing to extend to him.

If he chose to accept it.

Deep inside, he felt a tearing sadness; because of course acceptance was impossible.

But Mike had saved his best surprise till last.

When the conversation died down, Mike took Edith by the hand and, shyly but proudly, announced she had agreed to be his wife. Amid congratulations and good-natured teasing, Edith produced the champagne she'd chilled in readiness to toast their engagement.

Although taken as much by surprise as the others by the timing of the announcement, Megan was not altogether caught out by their news. She'd observed their long-term friendship growing steadily warmer, especially since her father's heart attack. Stifling the pang of envy that lanced through her own wounded heart, she congratulated them sincerely.

Edith and Mike were right for each other, and Megan believed they would be happy together.

'This is their time,' she lectured herself sternly. 'I won't spoil it for them by moping over my own shattered dreams.'

When the hubbub died down, Mike sat beside Jon to tell him about the furnished flat above the garage. It was his if he wanted somewhere more private than his room at the Victoria.

"It needs to be lived in, so you'd really be doing me a favour," Mike urged. "After the wedding, I'll be moving into Eddie's house. Until then, I'll stay with Meggie. Too many steps up to the flat, Doc says, so if you like, you can move in immediately," he offered.

It was an appealing idea.

Jon was fed up with the hustle and bustle and lack of privacy at the hotel, friendly though everyone was. For the remainder of his time in The Crossing, he might as well be comfortable.

"That's very generous of you, Mike," he said. "I'll take you up on it." Meeting Megan today, face to face at last, hadn't been the ordeal he'd feared. Perhaps he'd been exaggerating the situation. Maybe the two of them could be friends after all.

'It's worth a try,' Jon promised himself.

~~~~~

It was a triumphant pair of middle-aged lovers who strolled arm-in-arm round to Edith's house later that evening, reviewing the results of their strategy along the way.

Megan had been cool, but politely friendly towards Jon, who, although also cool, had been less stand-offish than usual. Also, he had accepted the flat.

So much more home-like, more settled, than a hotel room, Edith maintained. That surely represented considerable progress, because if Jon was really set on leaving, why bother?

"Maybe Jon has a subconscious desire to stay," Edith speculated, hoping it was so.

It was an added bonus that now, only a garden fence would separate the young people. Edith anticipated a good many accidental meetings in the future, each one leading to a better understanding between them.

Jon hadn't accepted the permanent job. Neither Edith nor Mike had expected him to at this stage, but he hadn't jumped to refuse it, either.

~~~~~

Arriving the next morning to help Mike clear the flat of his personal possessions, Edith brought a hamper of home-baked goodies to see Jon over the remainder of the weekend till the shops reopened on Monday, overwhelming him with her kindness. Megan, simultaneously resigned and secretly excited against her better judgement, to Jon's full-time presence next door, pitched in too, vacuuming and dusting. Not that much work was needed since she'd been keeping the flat clean and tidy, ready for its owner's anticipated return.

After a great deal of serious thought, Megan had decided that in the circumstances a coolly polite neighbourliness towards Jon would be her best policy.

Neither of them would be embarrassed that way, and more importantly, neither would her father be upset by churlish behaviour on her part.

It took a remarkably short time to install Jon in his new home.

Edith and Mike had left with a car load of items being taken directly to Edith's house, when Jon stopped Megan as she was about to retreat to her own side of the fence.

"Megan, I owe you an apology."

'What for,' Megan thought rebelliously. *'For breaking my heart?'* However, she maintained her bland surface composure and heard him out.

"Last weekend, when I kissed you in the garage," Jon flushed awkwardly and rushed on.

"I had no right to do that, Megan. I behaved like an animal, grabbing you like that."

The fact that he wanted to do exactly the same again, right here and now, was something he was determined to ignore. Getting involved with Megan Patterson was simply too dangerous to even be contemplated.

He forcefully quelled the urge to act on his desires and continued with his prepared spiel. "You deserve better. A lot better. I forgot about Bob, as well. Can you forgive me, Megan? Is there a chance we could be friends in future?" Both embarrassment and desire gave way to a vague anxiety, his eyes pleading with her while he waited impatiently for her answer.

"Bob?" Megan seized on the least important aspect of this surprising apology. "What does Bob have to do with us?"

"Aren't you planning to marry him? Angie said the whole town's expecting it."

Megan saw red. How dared he gossip about her, and with Angie Wilson of all people!

"Well Angie's rather inaccurate with her information and I just hope she's not spreading that silly story all over town," Megan informed him tartly.

Annoyance added a shrill overtone to her usual gentle speaking voice. Hearing it, she reined in her anger to continue more mildly. "I admit we did briefly toy with the idea quite a while back. But we weren't in love with each other, so gave it up by mutual agreement. Marriage between us would have been a mistake. Not that that's any business of Angie's, or anyone else's, so don't you go spreading it around."

The suddenly squelched brightening in Jon's grey eyes made Megan's wayward heart skip a beat, although she went on placidly enough, the uplift to her own emotions strengthening her control over her vocal tones.

"As for the rest of your apology, it was rather an ego boost to discover you could get so carried away with *me,* so I guess I can forgive you." Of course she forgave him. Hadn't she known she'd do just that if he gave her sufficient excuse? "You weren't alone, you know, only I'm not going to apologise for it." Let him make what he liked of that bold admission. Truth, even if not the whole truth, was better than a mealy-mouthed, simpering denial of the passion that had flared between them.

"Of course we can be friends," she added casually, almost as an afterthought.

Neither mentioned Jon's behaviour at the dance, both feeling uneasily that some things were better left alone.

"Then why don't you come with me now, down to the Victoria. Let me buy you a drink to seal our friendship?" Jon regretted the impulsive invitation as soon as the words left his mouth, but it was too late to retract it.

Megan stared at him, mouth slightly agape. Heart aflutter, she heard herself accepting instead of uttering the refusal hovering on her lips.

If Jon seriously wanted to be friends, she'd meet him half-way. This time she wouldn't let wishful thinking lead her into misreading the situation, but didn't friendship sometimes grow into love?

It seemed room for hope still existed.

Entering the bar, they were greeted by a happily smiling Angie Wilson. Megan had almost forgotten about her, and stiffened, forcing herself to relax again.

"Hello, you two," Angie called out. "It's good to see you again Megan. I've been thinking I'd give you a call and we could meet up for a coffee one morning if you like. What's wrong, Jon? I thought you'd left us. Can't you tear yourself away?" Angie's unaffected laugh indicated nothing deeper than casual friendship between the two of them.

Returning Angie's greeting and agreeing vaguely to a coffee morning, Megan congratulated herself on her sang-froid.

She had felt rather uptight at meeting Angie, but the other woman hadn't acted as if Jon meant anything special to her. Neither had Jon appeared to take any particular notice of Angie, merely ordering the white wine Megan asked for, and 'the usual' for himself.

Could she have been wrong about them?

When Megan put her jealousy aside and considered what she'd observed, coolly and objectively, she discovered room for more than one interpretation.

She'd have to think carefully before jumping to conclusions, however the sun appeared to shine more brightly all of a sudden.

Megan raised a quizzical brow when a can of Pepsi was placed in front of Jon.

"The usual?"

Grinning back at her, relieved to be on such easy terms after all his agonising, Jon answered more freely than usual.

"Alcohol and bikes don't mix. I used to be a fairly heavy drinker. Drowning my sorrows. Until a friend I used to ride with killed himself one night on a wet road. I still like a beer as much as the next man, only now I'm careful to stick within reasonable limits, especially if I'm planning to hit the road."

A friend's death was a tragedy, only the more Megan turned the story over in her mind, the more she was convinced it wasn't enough on its own to have driven Jon into becoming the loner he now was.

If she was patient, maybe he'd eventually share more of his personal history with her. In the meantime, she'd make the most of their detente. No romantic nonsense though. No way did she intend to expose herself to another painful rejection. Friends was what the man asked for. Friends was all he'd get. Unless their circumstances changed radically.

~~~~~

Walking home together some time later, Megan felt relaxed, at ease with Jon as never before now her false expectations were dispelled. She still loved him. The difference was, now she knew for sure Jonathon Armitage wasn't ready to love her back and maybe never would be. Although he did seem to enjoy her company today, it still wouldn't be safe to trust her happiness to a man who was more interested in leaving than staying. With these thoughts running through her mind, Megan impulsively turned to Jon.

"I do wish you'd do as Dad wants, Jon, and stay on permanently. You fit in so well, here in Oxley Crossing. If there's nowhere else you really need to be, couldn't you give it a try?"

The comfortably relaxed man at her side bristled into instant hostility.

Jon stopped abruptly and turned to face Megan.

A frown now darkened his brow, lips tightened, and Megan noticed hands curling into fists at his sides.

Silently cursing herself for her stupid clumsiness, Megan rushed to repair the damage.

"It's none of my business, is it? Don't mind me and my big mouth, Jon. I was thinking of Dad, not you. You know what's best for yourself, so I'll try not to be pushy."

Her palms held upward, Megan smiled apologetically, breathing a sigh of relief when Jon shrugged, fists eased back into open hands, and the forbidding glare faded.

Megan walked on, chattering inconsequential nothings; monosyllabic responses her companion's meagre contribution to the conversation.

~~~~~

Jon still found Megan altogether too enticing for comfort, but forewarned by experience of how volatile their physical responses to each other could be, he grimly controlled his impulses.

Friends, he reminded himself. Just friends; no more.

He was sure he could handle being friends for the remainder of his short, hopefully very short, sojourn in The Crossing. However, the dangerous attraction Megan held for him lent an added cachet to their chance encounters, drawing him irresistibly into her orbit.

He would need to keep his wits about him, he reminded himself, then went right on thinking of her and recalling the heady sweetness of their one hot, wild kiss.

A kiss he itched to repeat, regardless of all his good resolutions.

Had Megan enjoyed his company as much as he had hers? Maybe she had. She'd asked him to stay on, hadn't she? For her father's sake or maybe her own? Jon wondered.

Didn't matter. Either way it was out of the question. He shied away from the implications of the warm glow of pleasure he felt because Megan liked him. Not even his boorish behaviour last weekend had turned her against him.

Reheating the casserole Edith had left for him, he couldn't help speculating. Megan wasn't involved with Bob any longer.

Even though he knew he was playing with fire, he wondered whether she might consider spending some time with him? Just as friends. He continued to mull over the possibility while he ate, failing to notice his need to remove himself from Oxley Crossing was losing its urgency.

Oddly content, happier than at any time since his arrival, Jon explored his new domain, admiring the bright, easy-care furnishings that encouraged relaxation. Mike's flat enfolded him in warmth and comfort; welcomed him like home.

~~~~~

That weekend marked a turning point for Jon. Life in Oxley Crossing was easy and pleasant and nothing untoward occurred to impinge on his peace of mind.

Also, he discovered living next door to Megan held a pleasantly unexpected bonus.

While he sat on the back steps with his morning coffee, he was treated to a minor strip show when Megan returned from her daily swim. She invariably made the clothesline her first stop, striping off the damp track suit she wore over wet swimmers, and hanging it and her towel to dry.

The first day he was there, Jon cynically assumed the display was for his benefit. Later, though, noting Megan never once so much as glanced in his direction, he concluded he was mistaken. But he continued to watch for her each morning.

The more he saw of Megan Patterson's neat, slender shape, the more he admired it and wondered why he'd never before realised that voluptuous, obvious attractions held less appeal for him than Megan's more subtle charms.

Megan had, in fact, been totally aware of her audience from the first, deigning it beneath her dignity to change her habits. Let him look. Maybe then he'd be less likely to forget her in a hurry. If she saw him later in the day, she'd wave and call out a brief comment or two, without interrupting the task she was engaged upon, making it quite clear to him she was in no way pursuing him. Pretending an indifference she certainly didn't feel.

As he became more settled, Jon soon began venturing down to the fence, prolonging their brief exchanges into amicable chats. One afternoon, seeing her struggling to dig a new garden bed, he surrendered to impulse.

"That job's too heavy for you, Megan," he called out as he ventured into her garden.

"Let me have that," he added, plucking the spade from her unresisting hands. Digging completed in considerably less time than it would have taken Megan, Jon looked up, wiping sweat from his brow, to find her waiting with an ice-cold can of Pepsi.

"Thank you, Jon. I really miss having Dad's help in the garden. Here, you sit in the shade with this while I get these seedlings planted."

After his hard slog, Jon was a bit disconcerted to be relegated to the sidelines, all but ignored.

Why was he feeling put out when Megan was doing exactly as he'd asked? Being friends.

Cool, keep-your-distance friends.

The night Mike invited him to join them for dinner was the same. Megan welcomed him, then practically ignored him, leaving most of the conversation to Edith and Mike.

Jon wasn't to know Megan had an ulterior motive in playing it cool. He merely assumed she wasn't interested. Suited him. Mike would find someone else any day now, then he'd be on his way.

'Strange,' he thought. Now life was just the way he wanted it, why didn't he find it as satisfying as he ought to?

~~~~~

Following their visit to the Victoria, Megan had concluded it would do her no good to throw herself at Jon. Probably the exact opposite if the night of the dance was any indication.

She hadn't reached her present age without having seen enough to learn men usually took what women offered.

Often thoughtlessly, without considering a girl might be seeking a life-long relationship, not simply enjoying the fleeting pleasures of an affair. Too many of her friends had been hurt in this manner, reinforcing her decision to wait for the right man. The man she was now convinced she'd found in Jonathon Armitage.

An affair with Jon was tempting, but would necessarily be brief if he was still set on leaving town; a decision he hadn't changed as far as she knew. An affair was doomed to end in heartbreak for her, almost before it began. The alternative?

'What do I really want?' As often as she asked herself this question, Megan arrived at the same answer. She wanted it all. And she wanted it with Jonathon Armitage.

She hadn't known him very long, but she intuitively recognised him as a sensitive man. A man whose word, once given, could be relied on. He stirred her deeply, lighting up her life and arousing hitherto unimagined desires; opening up wholly new dimensions of experience to her.

Jonathon Armitage made her feel like a woman, with all of a woman's needs.

He was more than a mere good-looking hunk. He was her soulmate. The man she wanted as husband, lover, father of her children and best friend.

Megan loved Jonathon Armitage. It was as simple as that. And as frustratingly difficult.

Was the strange, enlivening energy flow she experienced at his every touch, her body instinctively recognising and responding to its mate?

That idea gave her a warm, comfortable feeling of absolute certainty. Only nothing was solved. Nothing was certain.

Unfortunately, except for that one wild, overwhelming kiss, Jon had never indicated he found her any more attractive than he found Edith!

He appeared quite content with their casual encounters.

Friends he'd asked for, so friends he'd get.

But if he ever offered her some positive encouragement, Megan vowed to be ready.

~~~~~

Edith and Mike, watching the young people closely, had revised their strategy several times.

However, they both loved Megan dearly, so reluctantly concluding they would be unwise to take any further affirmative action, they awaited developments. They'd done all they could. For now.

The next move belonged to Jonathon Armitage. If he committed himself to becoming a permanent resident of The Crossing, time would be on their side. And Megan's.

They crossed their fingers and prayed. And waited impatiently.

~~~~~

Another week dawdled by. Jon questioned Mike about replies to his ads, only to be told sadly that no-one had replied yet. He shook his head, exasperated with the older man.

"You know, Mike, I reckon you wasted your money with those ads you put in the papers. They could have been worded a lot more effectively."

"Go on." Mike nodded apprehensively.

Was Jon about to hand in his notice again? The sick old codger routine wouldn't work a second time since Jon was now fully aware of his excellent progress. Eddie would skin him alive if he let their prey escape at this point. He listened closely as Jon explained.

"You didn't say anything to attract a serious applicant's attention, Mike."

For some reason, Jon had found the simple advertisement offensive in its brevity.

"How can you expect anyone to know what a good offer it is? You ought to redraft the ad. Dangle the possibility of future prospects as an incentive. Perhaps something like the possibility of leasing the garage instead of being a mere employee. Isn't that what you meant when you offered it to me? Sell the town a little, too"

He gestured with his hands, as if trying to encompass the whole town in them.

"It's a great little place, Mike. You could promote it as a wonderful opportunity for a young family man."

Mike looked at him with interest, agreeing wholeheartedly with every word uttered.

Only the one man he wanted to attract was Jonathon Armitage himself. Cautiously, he eyed Jon, wording his next question very carefully.

"Do you really believe that, Jon? That Oxley Crossing is a great little town? I was under the impression you didn't think much of us. Ever since you arrived, you've been itching to leave."

"Of course it's a great place. The people too. It didn't take me long to realise that, Mike. But it's a place for putting down roots, and that's just not me. I've never been comfortable in one place for too long. Didn't Megan tell you I'm a drifter?' His lips twisted bitterly on his last words.

"She did. Jon, I know you've been a drifter. So was I a long time ago. Then I met my Jenny." Mike smiled fondly as memories flitted through his mind. Jenny had been a fine girl who'd led him a lively dance until he won her love. "Settling down came naturally then. It could be easy for you too, you know. If you wanted to give it a try."

At the risk of sticking his neck out and getting it chopped off, he went a step further in his argument.

"Out here, we're a long way from whatever you're running from, Jon; and you must be getting mighty tired of running." Mike took a sidelong look at Jon.

"Ever considered it might be time to stop?"

The arrival of the electrician to install new kitchen equipment for the cafe brought the uncomfortable discussion to an end.

~~~~~

Damn Mike! He was talking through his hat. Lips compressed angrily, Jon wasted no time escaping to his own domain, thoroughly disturbed and out of sorts.

For days after, no matter how hard he tried to wipe them from his mind, Mike's words returned time after time at unexpected moments, until Jon found he was no longer dismissing them out of hand.

Could he settle down? Here in The Crossing? He didn't know, and was sure he wasn't ready to find out. It had been easy for Mike because he had his Jenny, but Jon had no-one.

An image of Megan's smiling face flashed through his mind, only to be thrust aside as Jon abruptly slammed the door on that errant thought.

Thoroughly unsettled, yearning for something he absolutely refused to even try to identify, Jon swore again.

Damn Mike and his crazy ideas. He had to get out of here. Soon. He cast a desperate glance in the direction of his Harley, parked in the far corner of the garage out of the way.

SAVING JONATHON ARMITAGE

10

Another Monday morning.

Jon yawned contentedly as he dragged himself out of bed.

The fine weather was holding, and although the farmers were casting worried eyes towards the cloudless sky, uttering dire predictions of drought, the sunshine had brought a bumper crop of visitors to Oxley Crossing over the weekend.

Mike's new cafe had had its first customers hungry for hamburgers and chips.

Business had been brisk, Mike and Judy almost run off their feet. He'd escaped on Sunday when Alan called, inviting him to spend the day at the farm.

He'd had a good time out there, mucking about with Alan and his kids. Jon smiled at the memory. Melanie and Jocelyn had fussed over him, demanding rides on the Harley and showing off on their Peewees.

He'd been given a riding lesson; horses, not bikes, by Alan's father, Andrew Morgan, surprising himself when he'd done okay for a beginner. Well enough to ride out with them on one of the easier trails the Morgans were blazing in preparation for when their plans to take in paying guests came to fruition in the near future. The girls had gone too, trotting ahead on their ponies.

Back in the farmyard, along with the kids he'd fed the poddy calves and orphaned lambs their bottles of milk, laughing at their antics as if he were a kid himself.

Farming wasn't his scene, but a short visit made a nice change in his daily routine. He hoped he'd be asked again before he left. If he was still here at shearing time, that would be something to see.

A soft expression crept into his eyes when he recalled Melanie and Jocelyn begging him to read them their bedtime story. They were two great kids. Did Alan appreciate how lucky he was? A renegade image of kids of his own flitted into Jon's mind, to be ruthlessly expelled. Hastily thinking of other things, he finished up in the bathroom and went to fix toast and coffee for his breakfast.

'I'd better watch out,' he warned himself, *'or I could end up tied down with a family. And wouldn't that be a recipe for disaster if ever there was one?'*

It sure would be. He wasn't cut out to be a family man. He wasn't. Time out with Alan's girls was fun, but that was as far as it went.

The first thing to meet Jon's eyes when he hauled up the roller doors in front of the workshop was the outsize cardboard carton standing squarely in front of them.

Frowning, he stared at it. It hadn't been there last night when he put the Harley away. Odd snuffling whimpers came from the box as he bent to investigate. Peering in, he drew back, annoyance shattering his good mood.

A dog! Some irresponsible fool had dumped a puppy on his doorstep. Didn't they know there were better ways to find a home for an unwanted pet?

Catching sight of him, the pup stood up against the side of the carton, yipping eagerly and wagging a ridiculously long tail. It was probably hungry. Poor little tyke. It didn't even have the advantage of being pretty. Most likely it was the last of the litter; the animal no-one had wanted.

'So they dumped it. On my doorstep.' Jon swore mildly, concern for the animal stronger than his annoyance. Now it was his problem.

Frowning, he realised he had little idea of puppy care. When they were kids, he, Gordon and Carolyn had had a dog, but he couldn't recall looking after it.

Their mother had done all that was needed. They had only played with it and taken it for walks. He'd really missed it when it died. He recalled his anger at their father when he vetoed getting another dog.

One cause of conflict among many.

He supposed the first thing he should do was feed it. This young, it might still drink milk. Perhaps with some bread soaked in it. That was about the best he could offer at this time. He'd feed it. Then get rid of it. Someone in town must want a pup for their kids.

Jon reached into the box, gingerly picking it up, getting his hands thoroughly licked as soon as they came in range of its sloppy pink tongue. The pup wriggled and squirmed, emitting excited, squeaky little barks. It did more than that. As Jon lifted it up, it piddled in its excitement, wetting the sleeve of his overalls. Swearing pithily, he dropped it back in the box. He wouldn't make that mistake again!

Next time, he picked it up carton and all, carrying it through to the back and up the stairs to his flat. During the night the rags lining the bottom of the carton had become wet, so, leaving the pup in its box on the landing outside the door, he fetched some of the tatty old towels Mike had used as cleaning rags. They'd suffice for fresh bedding. Now for that bread and milk.

In short order, Jon was sitting on the top step watching the pup wolfing down its breakfast. Looking up, he saw Megan wander out her back door.

"Hey. Megan," he called impulsively. "Come on over here. I've got something for you." She looked up, brow raised at his peremptory tone. He grinned, adding a belated, "Please, Megan."

Smiling craftily to himself, Jon decided Megan was the ideal person to adopt the pup.

She was sure to know how to care for it, and, with her soft heart, she really ought to have a pet. Eyeing the unprepossessing animal, Jon rehearsed his spiel, assuming an air of innocence. Megan was a soft touch, always fussing over other people's animals. If he played his cards right, she'd be tickled pink to have this puppy for her own.

Wrong. Jon's salesmanship had failed him.

Megan had been and gone and here he was, still in possession of the pup. It would have to wait; his work wouldn't do itself. Next thing, he'd have Mike yelling up the steps wanting to know where he was.

Working quickly, Jon constructed a rough pen on the back lawn next to some shady bushes. He retrieved the pup from its nature ramble in the garden, then, careful how he handled it, he put it in the pen along with the freshly lined carton; lying on its side now to allow the pup easy access. A bowl of water, and it was on its own.

~~~~~

Poor Jon.

Megan chuckled as she walked back through the connecting gate. He'd tried so hard to persuade her to take that pup. She hadn't been able to resist teasing him a little, pretending she might be interested.

That poor pup. It looked such a clown with its short legs, long feathery tail, droopy ears and pirate patch over its left eye. The rest of its coat was white, with black socks on the two hind feet.

Probably it would have rough hair when its adult coat grew in. A long way from a respectable pedigree, yet oddly appealing. Jon had looked so delightfully helpless.

"No Jon, sorry. You've got a cutie, but I'm not in the market for a pet. Especially not a pup I'd have to spend a lot of time training. Look, she adores you already. You're the one who should have a dog, not me. Just think of all that unconditional adoration." She laughed. They made a comical pair, Jon and the pup.

The temptation to detour via the cafe to share the joke with her father and Jack was irresistible.

They made an appreciative audience, both of them as amused as she'd anticipated at the thought of the self-contained Jonathon Armitage having to cope with a young pup. Megan wouldn't let the poor animal suffer; she'd give it a home herself, first, but she really did believe it would be good for Jon. Another life besides his own to be responsible for. The reward - a loyal, loving companion. Puppy love. Megan was still grinning when she settled behind her desk.

Her father and Jack agreed with her wholeheartedly.

"Do him good to have something to worry about besides himself," Mike said.

"Make 'im a bit more human, know what I mean?" Jack had summed up in his laconic drawl. "That boy needs to loosen up a bit."

Neither of them would lift a finger to help him offload it, not unless it became a question of the little dog's welfare.

But Megan knew Jon would never let it come to that. She'd seen the gentle way he stroked it and the soft glow in his eyes as he fondled its floppy ears.

A helping hand couldn't hurt though.

Checking her diary, she saw she had no appointments till ten o'clock. The eternal paperwork would keep a few minutes longer. She grabbed her purse and scooted down to the shops. In double quick time, she was in the garage, tapping Jon on the shoulder where he was bent over with his head under the bonnet of a car.

Her breath came fast, a blush warming her cheeks beneath her light make-up, as she recalled the last time she'd bearded Jon in his workplace. But this was no time for banned romantic memories. She swallowed hastily, narrowing her focus to the matter in hand.

"Puppy food. Six cans, assorted flavours. See you later," Megan informed Jon. Dumping the bag on the bench, she raced out.

"Thanks Megan. That's terrific," drifted after her. "Terrific," Jon repeated to the dusty air, now smelling enticingly of spice and flowers. "Just terrific. If she's going to buy food for it, why can't she take it and look after it herself?" He shrugged. At least now he had something more appetising to offer it than bread and milk.

Before he returned his attention to his job, he ambled outside to check up on the pup. Smiling at its exuberant welcome, he ruffled its coat and tickled it under the chin.

"Megan brought your lunch, Pup. Maybe if we keep working on her, she'll give in and take you home with her next time."

With a last pat, Jon returned to work, whistling a popular tune.

~~~~~

Mike hadn't waited long before ringing Edith to share the news, sure she'd get a kick out of the image of Jonathon Armitage as foster parent to a homeless pup.

Her reaction was even more satisfying than he'd expected, leaving him basking in the comforting warmth of her approval.

"Brilliant Mike. Perfect. A dog's just the thing to settle him down. Now, be encouraging, only mind you don't let him palm it off on *you*. I know what a softie you can be, Mike dear."

Edith began turning over ideas for helping Jon without relieving him of one iota of responsibility for the dog.

"Ah, that's it," she exclaimed, hurrying off early to the library to see if the book she wanted was on the shelves. Yes, there it was. 'Puppy Training For Beginners'. Just the book to set Jon up as a responsible pet owner, with information on diet and general care as well as training techniques.

Entering it on Jon's card, she rushed it round to him before opening the library for business.

"Hello, Jon dear." Edith got his wary attention as she bustled in.

"Mike tells me you've got yourself a puppy. I thought you might find this book useful. Keep it as long as you need and don't worry about getting it back on time, dear. I know where to find it."

Thanking Edith for her thoughtfulness, Jon attempted to explain it wasn't actually his dog, but Edith waved his explanation aside.

"Cheerio then. You're busy, so I won't keep you," she said, rushing off as quickly as she'd come.

Flicking through the book, he noted it did indeed contain quite a lot of useful information. If you had a dog, which he didn't. He tossed it aside. He'd recommend it to whoever took the pup off his hands.

The phone had obviously been running hot.

When Jack's daughter, Susan, came on duty, she brought a leash and a small collar. Her children's dog had outgrown them; Jon could have them for his new dog. She brushed his thanks aside, hurrying off to serve a customer.

Lunchtime saw Jon making a trip to the shop himself, to buy food and water bowls. The make-shift plastic ones from the kitchen kept getting tipped over. That was his excuse anyway, when he asked himself why he was bothering since the dog wouldn't be staying. Reaching out he flipped a couple of puppy toys off their hooks as well.

Poor little brute. Jon was so sorry for it, he wasted a few extra minutes playing with it. He even let it out of its pen to run around the garden with him till he had to go back to work. A sight which had Megan smiling to herself from her kitchen window viewpoint while she prepared lunch.

It wasn't a bad little creature really, Jon thought. Very affectionate. Very grateful to be shown a bit of attention. This afternoon he'd try walking it on the lead. Probably it was too young, but he might strike it lucky and find someone who wanted it.

~~~~~

No such luck. Oh, Jon met plenty of people. People who'd fussed over the pup, laughing when he offered it to them.

"Free to a good home," he repeated about a dozen times.

The children who came to pat her threw him into confusion by demanding to know her name, surprised he hadn't given her one yet. Jon supposed she did deserve a name. Every pet did.

One with a bit of dignity, he decided, to offset her clownish appearance.

He picked up the pup, tired out from pulling and straining at the leash while being paraded around the park. Tucking her under his arm, he strode down the street, veering through Megan's gate instead of his own at the last minute.

Running her to earth in her vegetable garden, Jon marched straight up to her.

"Megan, I need your help," he demanded. "I'm told this animal needs a name, only I haven't a clue what sort of names you give dogs, except for Fido or Spot. I refuse to call her anything so hackneyed."

Amused by his defensive tone, Megan glanced up at Jon, observing the confident manner in which he held the pup in one large, strong hand, fondling it absent-mindedly with the other, and recalled how he'd almost had to force himself to hold it just a few hours earlier.

Tugging off her gloves, she gestured him to the garden seat, jealously imagining the heaven it would be if those large, work-calloused hands were fondling *her* with such satisfying thoroughness.

Using the dog as an impeccable excuse, she sat close beside him, leaning self-indulgently against his shoulder to reach over and scratch the pup behind the ears; dodging out of the way of its tongue with a breathless laugh.

"What kind of name do you have in mind, Jon? This is a dog with real character, isn't she? I guess you won't want a name like Cuddles or Snookums."

Jon suppressed a shudder. No, he definitely didn't want a baby name like those.

The two of them spent the next half hour hilariously topping each other's ridiculous suggestions. Both forgetting in the camaraderie of the moment to keep their distance from each other.

"Seriously though, Megan," Jon finally asked, "what about something like Trixie?"

"Trixie?"

Megan rolled the name round her tongue, experimenting with the sound of it. "Trixie. I like that, Jon. Hey, Trixie," she clicked her fingers, calling to the pup, "how about it then? Will we call you Trixie?" Tail wagging joyfully, the pup came racing up to them.

"I guess that's your answer, Jon," Megan chuckled. "She's responding to it already. Wait here and I'll fetch us a drink to celebrate. I'd invite you in, except our little lady here isn't house-trained yet." By the time she returned with the drinks, Mike had arrived.

"Hi Dad," she greeted him. "What do you think of Jon's dog? He's decided to call her Trixie."

"Nice choice, Jon. She looks full of tricks, doesn't she?" Mike commented, making no effort to hide his grin. Naming a dog implied ownership, didn't it?

~~~~~

Jon wasn't sure when he'd given up disclaiming ownership. It had just happened. Trixie was his dog now, and that was that.

They went home together to get their dinners and study Edith's book on puppy training. Following its instructions, Jon set about educating Trixie, and during the following days proudly showed off every new trick she learnt to Megan.

Jon was proud of his pet's quick intelligence; and sharing her triumphs with Megan seemed to come naturally.

By Saturday afternoon when Alan dropped by with his girls, an unbreakable bond had been forged between man and beast. It had been days since Jon last toyed with the idea of giving Trixie away. Today he was happy, playing with her in the garden while Megan worked nearby, weeding Mike's rose beds.

Melanie and Jocelyn came racing through the side gate their father held open for them.

"Uncle Jon! Uncle Jon!"

"Hi Uncle Jon. Can we see your new puppy?"

Without hesitation, they threw themselves into his arms, generously bestowing hugs and kisses which Jon returned with equal generosity. Jealously, Megan observed the warmth of Jon's affection for the children. Lucky girls.

Was this the same Jonathon Armitage who had until quite recently held himself aloof from everyone? Everyone except kids and abandoned pups apparently. Unfortunately, he hadn't shown any inclination to admit her into the magic circle.

"Ooh, look Daddy. Isn't Uncle Jon's puppy sooo cute!" squealed Jocelyn.

"Me first!" Unceremoniously Melanie elbowed her sister aside, only to be vigorously shoved back as Jocelyn refused to yield her position.

Megan exchanged quiet greetings with Alan, both of them absorbed in watching the clamorous interaction between man, children and dog. Jon finally tore himself away, strolling up to the two adults.

"They heard on the school grapevine you had a new pup," Alan laughed. "I had no peace till I agreed to bring them to see her for themselves. Girls! Manners," he called loudly.

Noticing Megan at last, Melanie and Jocelyn ran over to give her a quick hug and kiss, rushing straight back to grab Trixie again, patting her and rubbing her tummy when she rolled over obligingly. About to retreat to her own side of the fence, leaving Jon alone with his visitors, Megan's intention was foiled when Alan wrapped an arm round her waist, pulling her down to share a seat with him.

"No need to rush off Meggie," he said. "Why don't you sit here and fill me in on the latest town gossip while Jon runs along and puts the kettle on."

His sidelong glance took in Jon's quickly suppressed frown when he'd claimed Megan's company. Interesting. Was the wind blowing in that direction?

Alan tossed the other man an insouciant grin. A dog; and Megan as well? Had Jon changed his mind about moving on? Alan couldn't resist a little discreet probing when shortly they were all sitting comfortably round the barbecue table with the drinks Jon had obediently fetched.

"How does Trixie take to the bike?"

Jon bit back a short laugh, resting sober eyes on his pet for a few seconds before answering reluctantly.

"She hates it," he finally admitted. "It's okay till I start up, then the noise terrifies her. I guess it'll take a while to train her to ride with me."

"So you do intend to take her with you when you go? Have you considered the sort of places where you usually stay? They don't often welcome pets. Maybe you ought to stay put here in The Crossing where you have a job and quarters where she's welcome. If you do, I can always use an extra man on the cricket team since Pete can't always make it."

Reaching casually under the table to scratch Trixie behind the ears, Alan pretended not to notice the glowering silence with which Jon greeted his nonchalant comments.

Melanie had been listening though.

"You're not going away, are you Uncle Jon? You can't go away. We've only just got to know you."

She clung to his arm as if she could physically prevent his departure, distressed tears welling up in her eyes. Jocelyn dived in to support her sister.

"You gotta stay here, Uncle Jon. We love you. We don't want you to go away."

Jon looked from the girls to Alan, to Megan, his harassed expression begging them to come to his rescue.

Neither did. Both watched with interest, waiting for his answer.

Megan especially. The questions Alan and the girls were asking were the very ones she badly wanted to know the answers to but had been too afraid to ask. In desperation, Jon attempted to reassure the girls.

"I'm not going away right this minute, you know. I'll be here for a while longer, but I can't stay for ever. The Crossing isn't really my home, you know."

His answer failed to satisfy. Melanie pouted.

"You could live here for ever and ever, if you wanted to," she told him in hurt tones. "If you really liked us, you would."

"Don't you like us, Uncle Jon?" Lower lip trembling ominously, Jocelyn joined the attack. "I thought you did like us. We like you."

"I do. I do like you. Both of you. Truly. Alright then, I promise to think it over," Jon promised rashly. Anything to restore the smiles to their faces. He couldn't bear seeing them so upset.

Did everyone in this place want him to stay? Previously, there'd been no argument from anyone when he decided it was time to move on.

Perhaps he really should think seriously about staying.

But what if he stayed, and they changed their minds about him? He'd better stick to the plan and go, Jon decided. Only not yet.

Trixie wasn't up to travelling on the bike, and no way was he leaving her behind. Megan's flippant comment about puppy love came to mind, but he didn't care.

"No more now, girls. Uncle Jon has a lot to think about before he decides what he's going to do. Don't hassle him anymore, okay?"

Thankfully, Jon realised Alan was distracting the girls. "You can hassle him as much as you like next time you see him."

Alan winked at the girls, making them laugh. Making everyone laugh as the children ran off, making up lists of topics to hassle Uncle Jon with next time. Soon after, Alan took his leave.

"I'll see you at the dance tonight. Save the first waltz for me, Meggie." He kissed her affectionately, deliberately making the kiss more intimate than usual, waved casually to Jon, and was gone.

The monthly dance!

Jon cursed silently, scowling at Alan's familiar manner with Megan. He knew they'd been friends since childhood; still, he thought Alan should keep his kisses to himself. Wasn't he was supposed to be in love with Angie Wilson? A social peck on the cheek was one thing, but in his opinion Alan's kiss had overstepped the mark.

"Are you going to the dance?" Jon's abrupt tone surprised Megan.

"Of course. No-one misses the dances without a good reason." Chuckling, she added, "There's not that much entertainment available locally, in case you hadn't noticed."

Jon was still frowning.

"What's wrong? Don't you want to go? It's not compulsory, you know."

"Yeah, I know. I just don't feel very social."

'Tell me something I don't know!' Megan stifled her impulse to laugh.

They sat silently, each bound up in their own thoughts.

"I'll go if you go with me, Megan," Jon mumbled half-heartedly.

"Sure, why not. We might as well walk round together."

It wasn't the most gracious of invitations, Megan thought, although she'd agreed with outward placidity. Inside, her heart soared. Was this a date? Deciding to count it as one, she collected her gardening tools and sauntered home, secretly walking on air. The weeds could wait; she had some primping and preening to indulge herself in.

Megan had hidden her delight from Jon, but she was going to make very sure she looked her absolute best tonight.

Mentally she reviewed her wardrobe, selecting and rejecting rapidly until she remembered a rather special creation. It wasn't new, but Jon hadn't seen it. Most important, she always looked really good in it.

She crossed her fingers, breathing a silent prayer that she'd return home happier than she had from the last dance. Native caution urged her to tamp down her expectations, but nothing could squelch the excitement bubbling away inside her.

SAVING JONATHON ARMITAGE

11

Jon's eyes travelled slowly from Megan's head to her feet and back again.

"Very nice."

He didn't know much about women's fashions, but Megan's lilac and silver dress looked good to him. Better than good. He let his eyes rove appreciatively over legs rendered extra long and slender in high-heeled, strappy sandals.

Although only a mild compliment, it brought a sparkle of pleasure to Megan's eyes that made Jon glad he'd uttered it. She twirled round, letting him see the back view, then wrapped both hands around his arm as they set off.

Proud to arrive in her company, Jon swept Megan onto the floor for the first dance.

Naturally light on her feet, following Jon's lead easily, Megan enjoyed herself.

They both danced well, their steps fitting together effortlessly. When questioned, Jon laughingly confessed that his mother had insisted he attend ballroom dancing classes with his brother and sister. He'd complained at the time, however the fifty-fifty program favoured in Oxley Crossing made him grateful for his proficiency.

Megan remained at his side when the music ended, until Alan led her off for the waltz he'd claimed that afternoon. For the rest of the evening she danced with whichever of her friends asked her, while Jon performed his duty with the ladies. It gratified her immensely to have him drift back to her side whenever opportunity allowed, dancing with her several more times.

It was so hard not to act possessively when she longed to demonstrate to the whole world that in Jonathon Armitage she had found her heart's desire.

Walking home under a full moon, Megan was aware of Jon's contented mood.

She walked very close, stumbling a little in her sandals on the uneven surface so their hands brushed lightly, overjoyed when their fingers tangled together.

When she dared to curl her fingers cosily around his, instead of pulling away as she'd been half afraid he might, Jon tightened his grip. His steps slowed, and Megan leaned against his shoulder.

It seemed so natural, so right, to be taken in his arms on the doorstep and kissed goodnight. A sweet, heady kiss with a tantalising shadow of the power of their first kiss. A kiss that was way too brief.

All too soon, Jon put her firmly away from him, hurrying off without a word before Megan could gather her thoughts enough to invite him in.

~~~~~

Remembering the wildfire their first kiss had kindled, Jon had restrained himself, permitting no more than a fleeting pressure as his lips brushed across Megan's. Even so, it was nearly his undoing. The meagre taste he permitted himself left him aching for more. Gently but firmly putting Megan to one side, he stepped back, barely waiting to see her through the door before retreating to safety on the other side of the fence.

There was a magnetic quality to the energy flowing between them. A strong magnetic quality. The more Jon tried to pull away from Megan, the stronger his attraction towards her grew. If he wanted to make a clean break when the time came, he'd need to make a better job of keeping his distance.

Leaving. Jon's face darkened, a vertical crease corrugating his brow. Why was he the only one who could see he had to move on?

Running, Mike called it.

Jon's frown deepened. Running had a cowardly ring to it. He'd never thought of himself as a coward. Did all those who'd offered their friendship consider him a coward? Surely not, or why would they want him to stay?

This question of cowardice was very disturbing. Too disturbing. Jon shook his head, pushing it all to the back of his mind and went to bed, his restless sleep punctuated by disjointed dreams.

Peculiar dreams, confusing images of Megan, children he recognised in the strange nature of dreams as his own from the future, and old memories of his family.

Waking early, he felt thoroughly out of sorts. Seeing to Trixie's needs, he put her into the garden and took the Harley for a long ride to blow the cobwebs out of his mind.

~~~~~

Waking equally early, but in a far more cheerful mood, Megan heard Jon ride out, wondering where he was off to so early. Last night had outstripped her meagre expectations. Lying back against her pillows, she relived the highlights. Their friends had turned the regular monthly dance into an impromptu engagement party for Edith and Mike, their happiness another cause for contentment.

'Only three more weeks till the wedding. I'll have to go to Tamworth next weekend, and find my dress.' Edith had asked her to be bridesmaid, and she had her orders to find a really special dress that would complement Edith's own.

Last night, Edith had had an extra surprise for the town. After she and Mike had been thoroughly congratulated on their engagement, Edith had taken the microphone to read a letter she'd received the day before.

The Tidy Towns judges had awarded Oxley Crossing second place for towns in their category. When the cheers died down, conversations broke out all round the hall, as people began discussing ways and means to do even better next year.

They knew Oxley Crossing deserved to win. Now they were even more determined to prove it to the rest of the country.

All in all, it had been one of the best dances Megan had attended.

Her thoughts grew more personal. Jon had danced with her five times! Angie had been present, but he'd only danced once with her. He'd danced with Megan, sat with her between dances, held her hand on the walk home, and kissed her goodnight. Megan hugged herself, not caring in the least that she was acting like a love-struck adolescent. Her ever-present flame of hope burned brightly.

Their kiss had been so brief. Over almost before it began. Megan's smile drooped. She'd ached with frustration, but now, in the clear light of day, she was more sanguine. The fierce intensity of their first kiss had scared Jon off. Almost right out of town.

Cool and patient was certainly proving more successful with her difficult love than hot and fast. Megan could hardly wait to see Jon later, to gauge his reaction to last night. Would he still be friendly and welcoming or would he have retreated behind that wall of icy reserve?

She'd find out soon enough. Along with Edith and her father, Jon had invited her to a barbecue lunch. Recalling her promise to bake his favourite chocolate cake for the occasion, Megan pushed back the covers.

It was time to pack away her daydreams and get busy.

~~~~~

The wind whistling past his ears sang a familiar soothing song. Jon's restlessness, engendered by hazily remembered dreams, was quickly blown away.

It was no more than an unconscious response to yesterday's talk, he concluded. Foolishly, he'd let it get to him. That, and Melanie and Jocelyn's distress. He could have done without their tears. Kids could really rip one up inside.

As for Megan's place in his dreams, that was easily explained. He wanted her, and he hadn't been with a woman for quite a while. Too long a while, obviously. No wonder a fleeting peck of a kiss had left him so frustrated and out of sorts. Another reason to be on his way. There was no-one in The Crossing to satisfy his casual needs.

That was the trouble with a place like Oxley Crossing. Girls were too serious about marriage. And marriage wasn't anywhere on his agenda. Not since his fiancée had jilted him.

Time to turn for home. He had a lunch to organise before his guests arrived on his doorstep.

In a return of hospitality, Jon had impulsively invited all three of them, Edith, Mike and Megan, to a barbecue. It had crept up on him how important their friendship had become to him, how much he trusted them and enjoyed their company.

It was almost like having a family of his own again.

While they sat talking after the meal, Mike suddenly sat up straight with a muttered curse. Fumbling in his pocket, he produced a sadly crumpled and dirtied envelope.

"Jon, I almost forgot. I found this earlier today where it must have slipped down out of sight behind the workbench. It's the letter I brought you ages ago. Read it this time, before you lose it again. Don't mind us, open it up and read it right now. There might be something important in it."

Jon turned the letter over and over in his hands, finally studying the sender's name on the back. It was from his sister Carolyn. The others tactfully cleared the table, returning the dirty dishes to the kitchen. Jon sat alone at the table, Trixie sleeping across his feet. Lost in thought, unhappy memories flooding his mind, he reluctantly summoned the courage to open Carolyn's letter.

He'd always got on well with his little sister. Jon smiled, remembering the way Carolyn teased him, calling him The Fonz when he'd ridden home on his first old second-hand Harley; so proud of himself in his black leather jacket and battered helmet. His smile faded.

That was before.

Carolyn hadn't been present when the final blow-up occurred and, unwilling to face further anger and disillusionment from yet another loved one, he hadn't waited around to say goodbye to her. He had no idea what she'd been told; how she felt about him.

He'd always assumed she'd side with their father and Gordon. Against him.

His heart broken by one angry row too many, he'd cut and run. And kept on running.

Jon admitted it to himself at last, shame a hot wire burning through his gut. Yes, he had run like the craven coward he was.

How had Carolyn known he was in Oxley Crossing?

And what could she possibly have to say to him after ten years? His heart missed a beat. Maybe Mike was right. This letter might contain important news. Bad news.

Slowly drawing the folded pages from their dirty, crumpled envelope, Jon began reading, his heart beating rapidly.

Dearest Jonathon,

I don't know whether this letter will reach you or not. Hopefully it will. When I put my car in for a service at Gino's, he told me a woman had rung him to check the reference he gave you. Knowing I would be interested, he jotted down her address for me. You were always good at your work, so I'm thinking positively and assuming you got that job.

Ten years is a long time, Jonathon. Much too long a time to be estranged from your family. Gordon and I have both missed you so much, wishing you'd return.

He told me what happened, but you know, he doesn't blame you at all. In his heart, he knew what Pam was like, and once he got over the shock, he realised you were innocent. Dad did too.

I never understood the bad feeling between the two of you. However, I do know that during the last ten years Dad has regretted it bitterly. He told me once he blamed himself for your leaving; that he'd been a terrible failure as a parent. I'm sure he would welcome the chance to make it up to you, if you would only let him.

Gordon is engaged again, to a girl called Susan Paulson. A very nice girl, and this time the two of them are truly in love and very happy. I'm engaged too. To Mark Simmons. Maybe you remember him. We're getting married on the twenty-ninth of next month.

I want you to come to our wedding, Jonathon. I want ALL my family with me on my special day. It would be a good time for you to return, and resolve old grievances. Lay them to rest forever.

Please come. If you have a wife and family, or a girlfriend, they're welcome too. Just make sure you come.

Please.

I love you, Jonathon.

Your loving sister, Carolyn.

Holding the letter loosely in his hands, Jon stared blankly towards the back fence. He couldn't go to her wedding of course, but how he wished he could. Especially if what Carolyn said was true. How he wished he could make it up with his family. As a child he'd always looked up to his older brother Gordon. Most of the time they'd been friends, and it had been Gordon he missed most when he left.

The one stinging accusation his brother hurled at him that night had hurt far more than his father's more vociferous anger.

Nothing he'd ever done had been good enough to please his father, and after his mother's death he'd given up trying.

Was Carolyn right? Was a reconciliation possible?

Believing he could never go back, he'd always barred such a possibility from his mind. Now the floodgates were opening on all his pent-up longings. At the gentle pat on his shoulder as a steaming cup of tea was slid in front of him, Jon looked up, sniffing back incipient tears. He focused blindly on Edith's concerned face.

"I won't pry, Jon dear. None of us will. But we want you to know we're here for you any time you need us. If that letter contained bad news, we might be able to help you."

Jon shook his head, struggling for composure. Edith really was so kind. In many ways she reminded him very much of his mother. No wonder he'd grown quite fond of her.

"It's not bad news Edith."

An uncertain smile flickered on his lips.

"The letter is from my sister. It's a shock to hear from her, that's all. I left home years ago, and this letter is the first contact with any of my family since then. She wants me to go home. She says they all do. I don't know what to do, Edith." He looked helplessly at her. "I don't want to leave here."

Where did that come from? Jon didn't know, but he was astounded to realise it was the truth.

"Then you needn't, dear." Edith answered gently as Mike and Megan, eyes warm and caring, brought their cups and rejoined him at the table.

"You're welcome here for as long as you like. Why don't you pay a visit to your family and come back again afterwards? How far away do they live?"

"Sydney. Yes, I could go for a short visit, I guess. Carolyn's getting married and wants me to go to her wedding. She says I should use it as an opportunity to make my peace. I can't, though. It's next weekend. There's not enough time."

"Nonsense, son," Mike interjected. "Of course there's time. It's only Sydney, isn't it? Not the other side of the country." Jon nodded.

"Okay then, get on the phone and ring her. Right now, Jon. Tell her you'll be there. It won't hurt to close the garage for the weekend, then if everything goes well, you can go again later, and stay longer if you like."

Jon shivered, goosebumps rising on his arms as he was swept up in the headlong rush of events.

"I think I do want to go, only I don't think I can face it alone. Carolyn said it's okay if I bring someone. Megan, will you come with me? Please? I really need your support."

Another astonishing truth. He'd think about that one later, too.

Honoured, yet taken aback by the unexpectedness of Jon's plea, Megan found herself lost for words. Not so Edith.

"Certainly Megan will go with you, Jon dear. Won't you, Meggie? We don't abandon our friends when they need us."

"Will you Megan?" Jon asked humbly, needing to hear it confirmed from her own lips.

Megan felt the last smidgen of resistance melt at the need so evident in Jon's face and voice.

"Of course,' she replied proudly, hanging on to her self-possession by a thread. 'You heard Edith. We don't abandon our friends."

While they'd been talking, Mike had quietly fetched his mobile phone. Now he pressed it into Jon's hand.

"You call your sister and sort it all out with her. You'll need to stay over for at least one night. Will you stay with your family? Get your sister to fix something up for the two of you."

Edith had been jotting notes, which she handed to him.

"Here's a list of things to organise with your sister for next weekend, Jon dear. I don't think I've missed anything important. Now, you phone her, as Mike said, then come over and tell us what's happening."

The three of them went through the gate to Megan's house, leaving Jon to phone Carolyn in private.

It was with a great deal of trepidation that he dialled the familiar number at the top of his sister's letter. Maybe she wouldn't answer, letting him off the hook. Part of him hoped for that, but the rest of him, by far the larger part, yearned for the chance she'd offered. When he heard her voice, scarcely changed over the intervening years, he was tongue-tied; so nervous he almost dropped the phone. Carolyn, thinking she had a hoax caller, was about to hang up when he finally found his voice.

"Carolyn? It's me, Jon."

"John? John who?"

"Jon. Your brother Jonathon."

"Jon! Is it really you? Oh, how wonderful. I'd almost given up hope of an answer from you. Oh, Jon, I'm so glad you called."

There was no mistaking Carolyn's pleasure, and Jon's fears evaporated. Suddenly they were both talking and laughing as easily as if it had been only days since they'd last spoken, not years. He couldn't believe how easy it had been. They talked for almost half an hour, until Carolyn, late for an outing with friends, called a halt. Now eagerly looking forward to next weekend's meeting, Jon sat replaying the conversation in his mind.

It was with an apology, he rejoined the others.

"I'm sorry Megan. I should have asked you first. There's a pre-wedding dinner after the Friday night rehearsal. I said we'd be there, only it means taking Friday off work to drive to Sydney. Can you manage that? If you can't, I'll ring back and say we can't make it."

"No need, Jon," Megan assured him. "I can reschedule my appointments. I do have one stipulation, though," she grinned at his apprehensive look. "Much as I'd love a ride on the Harley, I refuse to travel pillion all the way to Sydney. We'll take my car, and share the driving."

Relieved to be let off so lightly, Jon wasted no time agreeing. Impulsively, he smiled back at her. A glowing, heart-warming smile, holding nothing back. The butterflies in Megan's stomach which had been stirring restlessly all afternoon, threatened to fly right out through her open mouth.

Who'd have believed Jonathon Armitage could appear so carefree. So natural.

So totally concentrated on herself, Megan Patterson, whom he'd spent weeks holding at a distance?

"Did I hear you say you'd love a ride on the Harley?"

Megan gaped, unable to believe her ears. Especially when Jon elaborated on his comment by adding casually, "Why not right now? I've seen a helmet you can use in the back of the workshop. Go and get changed and I'll meet you out front."

"Yes, Meggie dear. You do that," Edith urged. "Mike and I have things we need to discuss. Off you go."

Glad for once to have the decision made for her, Megan hastened to obey, elated at the sudden upturn in her difficult relationship with Jonathon Armitage. She'd be certain to discover a lot about his past next weekend; then perhaps, she might be better able to understand the man; maybe even see the way clear to winning his love.

A huge maybe.

Mounted pillion on the Harley, Megan made excellent use of her unexpected opportunity to indulge herself. Slipping her arms round Jon's waist and clinging tightly, she snuggled up as close as she could, her tingling breasts crushed against his leather clad back. She was where her heart told her she belonged. Crossing her fingers for luck, she breathed an earnest prayer against another nasty letdown.

Jon adjusted his position, leaning back slightly into Megan's enfolding embrace. Wishing her arms wrapped so snugly around him were there for more than support. His body throbbed, too responsive to her presence for comfort. He wrenched his attention back to the road.

With such a precious passenger, he couldn't afford the distraction of wayward erotic imaginings.

Megan was going out of her way to support him next weekend, and doing it blind. It was especially kind of her considering his past treatment of her. He didn't deserve such generosity of spirit. At the very least, he owed her an explanation.

Sitting at the lookout on top of Dingo Hill, Jon steeled himself to tell Megan about the anger and unhappiness between his father and himself.

"I always felt he didn't like me. I was different, you see. Not good enough for him. I just couldn't be the son he wanted, Megan." Jon's eyes held a bleak expression that tore at Megan's heart. "Dad was ambitious for all of us; wanted me to go into the legal profession, or something along those lines. He refused to understand an office bound career wasn't right for me. I was a good enough student, but I hated being shut up all day in school. Couldn't wait to leave. No way could I ever have worked in an office."

Megan thought of all the times she'd heard Jon whistling as he worked on someone's faulty machinery; happy and contented, unconcerned about grease under his fingernails or oil stains on his clothes. He was right. An office wouldn't suit him.

"I always wanted a job where I could work with my hands. When I signed on with Gino as an apprentice, Dad nearly blew a gasket. It was Mum who calmed him down and persuaded him to give his consent. She was always the peacemaker. Even then, he kept on sniping at me."

Jon squirmed uncomfortably.

"No matter how good I was at anything he was never satisfied."

He heaved a sigh, running one hand over his face as if wiping away bad memories. Daringly, Megan laid her hand over his other one where it rested between them on the seat, offering silent comfort. Jon rewarded her with a faint shadow of a smile, turning his hand up to clasp hers loosely.

"After Mum died the conflict between us escalated until I stopped caring what he thought. When the final blow-up came, I just took off."

He lifted Megan's hand onto his lap, cradling it between both of his.

Instead of scaring him as it had previously, today their strange electrical chemistry soothed his troubled spirit; only he was too intent on his confession to notice.

"It was all my fault, that last row. Gordon was engaged to Pam, but I'd seen her out and about with other men behind his back. I tried to tell him once only he wouldn't listen. He kept on making excuses for her. Dad was no help either. She wound him round her little finger, so he thought she was the bee's knees. Since she came from a wealthy, well-connected family, he was all for the engagement. Megan, she was one of those women who aren't happy till every man in sight is her slave."

Jon's narrative halted abruptly, uncertain eyes pleading for Megan's understanding.

"Go on, Jon." Megan squeezed his hand, urging him to get the whole sorry story off his chest and out into the open.

"When she tried to come onto me, I decided to show Gordon, instead of just trying to tell him. Stupid, but I was too young and cocksure to know better. Gordon had rung to say he'd be home early. Pam didn't know, so it seemed the perfect opportunity to put my scheme into action. But like most of my good ideas it didn't go according to plan. I hadn't bargained for Dad's arrival with Gordon. All hell broke loose, with me cast in the role of villain. So I grabbed my gear and hit the road."

Jon lapsed into silence. This time Megan sat, equally silent, holding his hands compassionately while she mulled over his story.

"This Pam," she began tentatively.

Meeting no resistance, she ploughed on, trying to make sense of Jon's actions. "You say you weren't interested. You just played up to her to show her up for what she was?" Jon nodded. "Couldn't you have explained? To your brother if not your father?"

"Maybe." he shrugged. "I did try, but not very hard. Neither of them was prepared to listen, at least not right then. And suddenly something snapped inside me. I took off. For good."

"I guess that explains a lot about why you're so anti personal involvements," Megan mused, persistently trying to get the whole truth.

"There's more though, isn't there Jon? I'll listen if you want to talk, but I won't be offended if you don't," she assured him.

Jon had come a long way today. He'd really opened up, trusting her for the first time. She wouldn't push too hard and maybe have him withdraw into his shell again.

Megan waited.

After another long silence, Jon roused himself, surprising her when he confided further.

"I've told you the worst. Might as well go for broke and let you have the lot." Instead of making him feel worse, baring his soul to Megan had lightened Jon's burden, encouraging him to share more.

"There was a girl I met a couple of years back. Thought she loved me as much as I loved her."

Megan's heart contracted with a jealous pang, and she had to force herself to listen.

"We were going to be married, but at the last minute she dumped me. Went back to the man she'd been going out with before I came along. There have been other women as well, although not that many, and every time it ended badly. I'm just no good to anyone, so I decided to go it alone in future. When I let people get close, I just end up the loser."

Abruptly tossing Megan's hands aside, Jon strode over to the Harley.

"Come on," he called over his shoulder. "It's time to go back." Barely waiting for Megan to get settled he roared off, back to Oxley Crossing. Back to the safety of his lonely flat, unaware that behind his back Megan was choking back tears.

Tears for him, not herself.

During the following week, Jon's nervousness increased daily, his mood tense and brittle.

He half regretted his promise to Carolyn. Half regretted, also, opening up to Megan. He was afraid she'd read too much into it, expect more of him than he had to give. It was a huge relief when she remained her usual placid, friendly self. Not intruding, but always with a ready smile to bolster his fragile courage.

At heart Jon was glad Megan was going with him. It was a long time since he'd relied on anyone other than himself, and at first was wary of the comfort he derived from her support. When she made no attempt to take advantage of the change in their relationship, he gradually relaxed. With Megan at his side, he felt able to face the worst of dragons.

Not that Carolyn was one of his dragons. Jon had no argument with her. He'd gladly go to her wedding and he'd do his best not to ruin it for her.

As for anything more, that would be up to Gordon and his father. He didn't intend to go out of his way for either of them. Merely facing them again would be hard enough. He thanked God he wouldn't be alone.

Recognising that until the meeting with his family was over, Jon was too uptight to spare any thoughts or emotions for her, Megan resigned herself to an unobtrusive place in the background. She would be there for Jon if he needed her, without demanding anything of him for herself.

At this time.

There was only room for so much high drama at one time in anyone's life, and she correctly divined Jon's immediate need was for calm, soothing, friendly support. Later ...? Who knew what might be possible.

Jon could rely on her. Her love for him deepening day by day, Megan willingly served as his true friend.

12

On arrival at the motel where Carolyn had promised to book rooms for them when Jon refused to stay at the house, they found an apologetic note waiting. There was a big Rotary conference on over the weekend and the only room available had been a family suite divided into two bedrooms, bathroom and sitting area. Carolyn had booked it for them; hoped they wouldn't mind.

"Too bad if we did," laughed Megan, fighting the nervous flutter in her stomach brought on by the intoxicating thought of being so close to Jon for two days. Still, she tried to appear totally nonchalant.

"If it's all there is, it will have to do, won't it?"

Taking her comment at face value, and relieved by Megan's lack of concern, Jon agreed. Although, he would have been more comfortable with separate accommodations.

After spending several hours in her company on the drive, he was all too aware that Megan was no less of a temptation now than she'd ever been, and he feared his ability to maintain a safe distance between them if they spent too much private time in close proximity.

They were early at the restaurant where the dinner party was being held, so they settled in the cocktail bar to wait.

Very edgy, Jon worked overtime pretending indifference, but Megan couldn't help being aware of his growing tension. He sat where he had a direct view of the door, looking up every time it opened.

His sudden tautness and abrupt loss of colour signalled the waiting was over.

The door burst open, and the blonde young woman leading the party in hesitated, eyes searching the room. Spotting Jon, regardless of the quiet, exclusive atmosphere, she ran across the room calling out excitedly, to the amusement of the other diners.

"Jonathon! Jonathon, you came. You're really here. Oh Jonathon, I'm so happy."

Standing, unsmilingly cautious as he watched her exuberant approach, Jon braced himself, then, as his sister flung her arms around his neck, his restraint broke and he was hugging her back, eyes unabashedly moist.

Before he could utter a word, he was being ruthlessly hugged again, by a man so like Carolyn, Megan assumed correctly he had to be Jon's brother Gordon.

"You idiot, Jonno," he half sobbed, half laughed.

"All those years wasted. Why on earth did you have to take off like that? When I calmed down, I knew you'd been telling the truth. I knew you'd never betray my trust. I'd suspected Pam was playing fast and loose, but I was in denial. We could have easily sorted it all out if you hadn't gone off half-cocked and disappeared on us." He hugged Jon again, continuing more soberly.

"I've really missed you, Jonathon. It's so good to see you again at last. We thought you'd come home when you cooled down. When you didn't, we looked for you, but it was too late. You'd disappeared. Now you're back, we're not letting you get away again."

An older, grey haired man, obviously their father, was standing back, eyes devouring Jon with such naked, yearning pain Megan's soft heart went out to him.

'Please, God, help them both,' she prayed silently.

Released at last from his siblings' embraces, Jon looked up. Seeing his father watching them, his mouth tightened. For an interminable moment they simply stared at each other, neither capable of making the first move.

"Dad." Jon's nearly inaudible cry broke the impasse. The older man stumbled forward, both hands outstretched to his son.

"Jonathon. Jonathon, I'm so sorry. Please forgive me. It was never my intention to drive you away, and I've regretted it every day since."

Agonised tears streamed silently down his face as he waited for his son's response.

Slowly, almost in slow motion, Jon stepped forward and put his arms round his father, hugging him fiercely, his father clasping him tightly in return.

Megan released the breath she hadn't realised she was holding. They had a long way to go yet, but the first step, the most difficult one, had been taken.

Introductions over, everyone took their places round the long table.

Megan's tactful attempt to leave Jon alone with his family was thwarted when he gripped her hand tightly, refusing to allow her to leave his side. Having spent so long believing himself to be an outcast, he still felt ridiculously nervous, despite his warm welcome. He still needed a friend at his side.

In her heart Megan rejoiced at Jon's need of her; and that he wasn't afraid to show it.

With the willing co-operation of the other guests, a cheerful, festive air settled over their table.

At the head Carolyn and Gordon worked hard, drawing on happy childhood reminiscences to remind Jon that he belonged. That he was one of them, with a special place of his own in their family and in their hearts.

His father, saying little but never taking his eyes from his long-lost son, took Jon aside as the party was breaking up, and the two spoke earnestly together for some time.

Back at the motel, Jon confided in Megan over a cup of tea.

His father had surprised him, he said, telling him how he'd always felt inadequate in his dealings with him.

"He said he didn't understand me, Megan. I was different to the rest of the family. He didn't know how to talk to me without it coming out as criticism and spiralling into an argument. Later, he acted so autocratically because he'd been afraid I was wasting my potential entering a trade, instead of going to university." He sighed, regretting the wasted years and the misunderstandings which led to them.

He had been a high achiever, even though he'd claimed to hate school, and his father, a barrister himself, just couldn't understand his son's desire for a career as a mechanic.

"Mum urged him to back off, to let me do what I wanted, but all Dad saw was a wasted opportunity. When I came home with a motorbike, Dad said he'd felt threatened. He was afraid I'd end up getting in with a bad crowd. After Mum's death, our discord escalated without her calming influence until neither of us could talk rationally to the other."

Megan's heart ached for the lost, unhappy boy Jon had been. And for the father who hadn't been there for him when he'd needed him the most. She reached over and gave his hand a gentle squeeze.

Following Jon's flight from home, his father had taken a hard look at himself, coming to view himself as a failure; totally inadequate in his dealings with the son who'd been shaped in a different mould.

Now, he sought to atone. To try again to forge a relationship with Jon, as two independent adults on equal terms.

"I agreed to try, Megan. He wasn't the only one who made mistakes. We both did." Jon cast Megan an imploring glance, tacitly begging for her understanding.

She squeezed his hand again, nodding encouragement.

"I don't know if we'll ever be friends. There are still so many unresolved issues, but I want to try, and so does he."

"Oh Jon, I'm sure you're doing the right thing. At the end, the grief you both felt for your mother must have made the situation even more difficult. I'm so glad you're giving yourselves a second chance. You're a son any man could be proud of. I truly believe your father's sincere in what he says."

Megan's comforting words of approval were balm to Jon's wounded spirit, and he relaxed.

"Thank you, Megan. You're a true friend."

Eyes glowing brilliantly, he brushed a soft, careful kiss across her lips before saying goodnight and retreating hurriedly to his own room.

~~~~~

Happy dreams filled Megan's sleep, her characteristic optimism in full flower when she woke the next morning to find Jon still relaxed and at peace, smiling warmly at her across the breakfast table.

Agreeing to meet in time to go to the church together, they separated, each having errands to attend to. Megan, charged by Edith with finding the perfect bridesmaid's dress during this unexpected opportunity for a shopping trip in Sydney, was meeting her friend Genie Sullivan.

Laden with packages and glowing with excitement, she arrived back several hours later to discover Jon in conversation with his brother, Gordon.

"Dad and Caro were both tied up with last minute details, but I slipped my leash," Gordon explained. "I thought Jon and I could have lunch together before I have to do my duty in getting the groom to the church on time."

Megan had never seen Jon so happy and eager. The trip to Sydney was turning out to be a wonderful success story.

That afternoon everything went according to schedule. Carolyn, a radiant bride, was a respectable five minutes late walking down the aisle on her father's arm. The service was simple, but beautiful. The reception a masterpiece of organisation and timing. Jon was surely the most handsome of men, Megan thought, with his long hair neatly cut and dressed in a stylish suit acquired specially for the occasion.

Megan herself was made thoroughly welcome; while Jon's family and friends were almost as excited to be renewing their relationships with their black sheep, as they were congratulating the bride and groom. Not that Carolyn minded being upstaged by her prodigal brother. Nothing could dim her radiance when yet another of her dearest wishes had come true.

Throughout the ceremony, and afterwards at the reception, Jon kept Megan close beside him once again. Having to repeat his story over and over taxed his temper, and Megan's gentle presence had given him strength. Her sympathetic squeeze of his hand eased his tension every time he had to answer the same tedious round of questions yet again.

When his father took Jon aside for another long, private conversation, Megan relaxed, concentrating on enjoying herself. She liked Jon's family, and was relieved that they appeared to return her liking.

Their warm reception of her augured well for the future; if indeed she had a future with Jon, she was careful to remind herself.

Just because he was leaning on her at this difficult time didn't mean he wanted her around forever.

Later, Jon tore himself away from his family to dance the last few dances with Megan. His arms holding her close, he shared his elation over the reconciliation.

Heart filled to overflowing, Megan dared to dream. Freed from the emotional prison of his unhappy past, maybe Jon could now find it in himself to return her love. As they danced, she'd become aware of unmistakable signs of arousal. Jon still desired her as he had from the beginning. A first step to loving her, or merely lust generated by propinquity? Megan chose to believe the former.

She was flying high on a euphoric cloud of love, and the romance that was an integral element of weddings.

The glass or two of champagne she'd sipped had also contributed its mite to her relaxed, happy state.

~~~~~

Ready for bed some time later, Megan stood sipping a glass of water in the kitchenette when Jon, hair curling moistly from the shower, clad in nothing but bare skin and white cotton boxer shorts, emerged from the bathroom.

Disconcerted at finding her there, he hesitated in the doorway. Then, pupils dilating, he scanned Megan from head to bare feet, and back again.

Slowly.

He savoured the sight of her long, slender legs emerging from beneath the short, navy satin nightie with flimsy shoestring straps. He breathed deeply, sucking in the familiar heady scent of her favourite perfume.

Megan caught her breath at being so exposed under his heated gaze. Her body responded to the blatant desire on Jon's face, her nipples tightening and a rosy blush suffusing not only suddenly heated cheeks, but all the way down her chest until hidden by her skimpy, low-cut nightie. She swayed towards him, then steadied herself against the counter at her back.

Jon reached out to brush gentle fingers over her hair, her cheeks, her shoulders, questioning eyes holding her own.

Bemused, Megan stared back at him, too stunned by the heat coursing through her body to say a word.

Lips curling in a sensuous smile as if he was totally pleased with what he was seeing, Jon bent his head and slanted his mouth softly over her own, savouring the hot, sweet taste of her mouth flavoured with minty toothpaste, champagne and a deeper, indefinable flavour that he recognised instinctively to be all Megan.

And that was all it took.

Unheeding of the consequences, Megan threw her arms around his neck, succumbing to her long pent-up desires. She loved Jon, and right now Jon wanted her as much as she wanted him; and she would deny him nothing. Deny herself nothing.

The kiss deepened, igniting a blaze deep inside her just as their first kiss had.

She twined eager fingers through his thick hair.

With a shudder, Jon pulled Megan to him, his hands running restlessly over her back and shoulders as he poured all the longing he'd been denying into his kiss.

Megan felt a sensation of burning fire trailing in the wake of Jon's hands, and slid her body sensuously against his. Dropping lower, his hands tenderly cupped her neatly rounded bottom, rucking up the lower edge of the short nightie to heat the sweetly rounded globes of bare flesh beneath it.

Breaking the fusion of their mouths, Jon rained delicate kisses over Megan's brow and eyelids, down her cheeks to the sensitive skin of her neck. Trembling and gasping, Megan dug her fingers into his back, encouraging further exploration.

Jon surrendered to the fantasies he'd been fighting for weeks. He sucked and nibbled on an earlobe, his hands performing wickedly exciting tasks beneath the nightie.

Straining instinctively against him, Megan silently demanded more. Sought to recapture his mouth.

The rapture already burning fiercely in the depths of her being flared out of control, fuelled by the exciting friction created by the work-roughened hand now caressing her breast. Taut nipples peaked within covering satin setting her blood on fire.

Jon's rigid erection pressed achingly against her belly, and, seeking even closer intimacy she writhed against him, arousing him to greater urgency.

Jon slid down the satin straps, lowering his mouth to her bared breast.

Megan felt a flame of pure ecstasy engulf her senses, sinking to where an incredible smouldering tension was building until she felt she'd explode.

"Yes! Yes! Oh Jon, yes please."

Megan's gasped cries goaded Jon to greater intimacy.

He eased his hand between her thighs, stroking her hot moist centre. Her aching flesh convulsed, the core of her being a pool of molten lava.

The last vestige of rational thought fled leaving Megan floating in a glorious euphoria. She had never allowed any man to touch her this intimately, and was overwhelmed by the wonder of it.

Jon picked her up and carried her to her bed, laying her on top of the sheets.

Completely naked, but too lost in passion for shyness as she felt Jon's hot eyes devour her, Megan reached out, silently imploring him to continue his lovemaking.

Shedding his shorts in one swift motion, Jon joined her on the bed, stretching his long limbs alongside her own. Megan filled her eyes with her first sight of the glorious vision of her man's fully aroused, male body.

"Touch me Meggie," he growled.

Emboldened by his entreaty, Megan obediently followed her curious eyes with caressing fingertips, eagerly exploring his chest with its intriguing flat, brown nipples nested in light whorls of dark hair contrasting erotically with the smoothness of his tanned skin.

Her downward journey continued until her questing fingers were stroking lightly along Jon's hard, hot erection.

Encouraged by his trembling shudders and murmured endearments, Megan breathed in Jon's intoxicating male scent while allowing her lips to travel greedily over the territory so recently explored by her hands, revelling in the feminine power she'd never known she possessed.

Driven almost beyond endurance, Jon rolled Megan onto her back. Clasping her hands above her head he sank his mouth into hers, intoxicated by the sweetness of her taste. Embarking on his own voyage of exploration, he urged Megan on to greater and greater heights until, unable to wait any longer, he positioned himself between her thighs.

Lifting her to meet him, Jon entered her in one long, deep thrust. And met unexpected resistance. Megan cried out softly, tensing momentarily.

Jon reared back, partially withdrawing, shock momentarily dimming the passion in his eyes.

"Don't stop now, Jon." Megan gasped, her hands reaching up to pull him back to her. "Please don't stop. I want you Jon. Now. Please. Don't stop or I'll die."

Jon kissed Megan again, gently at first, then more fiercely, moving deeply within her.

Sighing her pleasure, Megan eased herself to accommodate him more fully, raising her hips instinctively to meet his repeated thrusts. Nature's eternal rhythm quickly established, her passionate response to Jon's skilful lovemaking brought her to a delirious climax.

Her world exploded, casting her dizzily into starry inner space, Jon following her over the edge of the abyss a moment later.

Reality was far, far more exhilarating than she'd expected. Unbelievably beyond what she'd anticipated.

Shattered by the sheer elation of at last giving and receiving love at the hands of her chosen mate, Megan felt joyful tears well up, spilling over to flow unrestrained down her cheeks. Overcome by emotion, she clasped Jon's sweat slicked body tightly to her own, his face buried in the hollow of her shoulder.

With words of love forming in her heart, she smiled tremulously when Jon roused himself to look guiltily into her face.

"Meggie, I'm sorry," Jon grated, rearing out of Megan's softly clinging arms at the sight of her tears. His own euphoria was instantly doused, overpowered by guilt.

Now he'd really gone and done it. He'd seduced Megan, his friend. Hurt her too, in his impatience, if her tears were anything to go by. She was lying there, crying. Regretting having given herself to him? His heart felt ripped apart and he turned his eyes away, unable to bear the sight of her pain. Their lovemaking had been all Jon had dreamed it could be.

Until he saw her tears.

His Megan had waited. Waited for that one, special love. Not for him! Never for him. His lips twisted in painful cynicism at the mere thought. He'd stolen a precious gift, never intended for him. Now Megan's dreams were irreparably shattered, leaving her lying there in tears. His fault. All of it his fault.

He'd mucked things up as usual.

And this time was the worst of all.

Snatching up his shorts, he rushed into his own room, where he flung on clothes with breakneck speed, too desperate for escape to bother with buttons, Jon rushed into the night. The last sound he heard as he pulled the door shut behind him was Megan's deep racking sobs.

Torn by guilt, he walked for hours, returning as dawn's pearly light lit the sky. How could he face Megan again? He couldn't face himself, let alone the woman he'd wronged.

If he'd had his bike, he'd have been long gone.

~~~~~

Rising early after a restless, broken sleep, Megan dived into the shower to wash away the evidence of the crushing heartbreak which had followed on the heels of rapture. Last night she'd wept bitterly when Jon left so abruptly. This morning she allowed anger to elbow grief aside.

She hated Jonathon Armitage, damn him.

How could he make love to her then rush off in such haste? As if he loathed the sight of her. Just a muttered 'I'm sorry,' then out the door. What was he sorry for?

Was he sorry he'd made love to her?

Sorry she'd been a virgin?

Both?

Not that the reason mattered. The result was the same.

Jon had turned her beautiful, loving, amazing, earth-shattering experience into something sordid and shameful. He'd thrown her innocent love back in her face, rejecting her cruelly.

At that moment Megan's fervent wish was to never see Jonathon Armitage again.

Showered and dressed, carefully applied make-up disguising the lingering traces of tears, she was struck by the silence from Jon's quarters in the front room of the suite. He'd raced outside when he abandoned her; putting space between them at breakneck speed. Through sobs she'd been unable to suppress, she'd heard the outer door shutting behind him. She didn't recall hearing him return, even though she'd barely dozed at all. Surely she'd have roused at the sound of the door opening and shutting. Wouldn't she?

Frowning, she peeped cautiously through the half open door of the front bedroom, noting Jon's unslept-in bed. He was gone. Devastated all over again, her heart plummeted, belying her angry wishes.

All his things were still there though. Megan looked around, puzzled. The key was on the kitchenette counter, exactly where she'd put it herself, beside the electric kettle.

Was Jon still absent? Because he'd locked himself out? Her heart began to race.

Curiosity, or maybe it was perverse hope, getting the better of her, Megan went to the front window, pulling the drapes apart to peek out.

Coatless, shivering in the early morning chill, Jon sat huddled on the doorstep; a picture of abject misery.

Sternly quelling her instinctive urge to offer comfort, Megan struggled to remind herself what a despicable rat he was. Deliberately she fuelled her anger as protection against further hurt.

Opening the door, she stood looking down at him dispassionately.

"The bathroom's free. You'd better get ready to check out if we're to join your father and Gordon for breakfast before we head back."

Expecting Megan to be as miserable as himself, maybe still teary-eyed, her icy self-possession acted on Jon like a douche of cold water. Angry his hours of self-flagellation had apparently been over nothing, he stalked past her without a word, heading straight for the shower, its moist steaminess evoking agonising images of a naked Megan, all wet and sudsy under the shower. Jon's wounded libido sprang into almost painful life and he swore under his breath. The fresh fragrance of Megan's particular perfume teased his nostrils, further inflaming his anger.

It wasn't till he got a closer look at her tense, white face while they loaded their cases into the car, that Jon realised how miserable and unhappy Megan was beneath her cool, poised exterior. His own anger melted away.

Somehow, although at the moment he had no idea how, he vowed to make amends.

He'd grown accustomed to being warmed by Megan's generous smile and it hurt unbearably to find himself deprived of it. Especially since it was the result of his own failings.

~~~~~

Breakfast at his father's house gave Jon and Megan both, a much-needed breathing space, since the necessity of maintaining a social facade helped defuse their fraught emotions. Megan was grateful the meal was served outdoors on the patio, allowing her to keep her sunglasses on. Leaving the conversation to the three men, she leaned back in her chair, lost in thought. Everyone was tired, so her withdrawn mood appeared unworthy of comment. With a long drive ahead of them, it was easy to get away soon after they'd finished eating, Jon leaving with a last promise to his father.

This time, he'd stay in touch.

~~~~~

An hour and a half later, well clear of Sydney traffic, Jon turned into a lay-by. Neither had spoken a word since they'd driven off, Jon at the wheel for the first leg of their journey. Megan, eyes still hidden behind dark glasses, roused from the unhappy reverie she'd fallen into to stare at him. Why had he pulled over in the middle of nowhere?

"We need to talk, Megan," Jon began, only to be interrupted angrily.

"There's nothing to talk about. You said it all last night. You're sorry. Well, you've no need to be. I may have been a virgin, but I'm not some naïve little girl. I won't embarrass you by expecting you to declare your undying love, or anything equally stupid." She might as well lay it straight out.

Wasn't attack supposed to be the best defence?

As long as Jon remained ignorant of her true feelings, Megan thought, hoped, she could cope with his rejection.

Jon winced at Megan's uncharacteristic sarcasm.

"You're so wrong Megan." Jon's sudden anger matched her own. "Last night *was* special for me. Very special. I care a lot about you. But you should have told me you were a virgin."

"It's done now, Jon." Megan cut in, wearily impatient with his fumbling excuses. "Let it go. I don't need a post mortem."

"But I wouldn't have been so rough, hurting you. I'd have made it better for you. Tried to, anyway." His words echoed in his ears, reminding him of what he was forgetting.

If he'd known Megan was a virgin, he'd have backed off at the very beginning, even if it killed him. There wouldn't have been any difficult discussion today. Lips tightening, he turned his head away.

Megan just stared at him for a long, uncomprehending moment, until angry words spewed out in a torrent.

"Nothing needed making better. It was already good for me. Really good. Until you went rushing off, making it clear enough what a terrible mistake you'd made, and that you couldn't stand the sight of me any longer." Megan's voice, rising stridently, wobbled dangerously on the last few words.

"That's not true Megan," Jon replied hotly.

"I was shocked when I saw how much I'd hurt you. Maybe not so much physically, but you were hurting emotionally. You were crying. I've never made any girl cry before. I felt so rotten. So ashamed. It wasn't you I couldn't stand the sight of. It was myself."

Jon wiped unsteady hands over his face, turning agonised eyes to Megan.

"I should have stayed to comfort you, only I was too big a coward. I did what I'm best at," he added bitterly. "I ran away."

During the silent drive, Jon had turned the disaster over in his mind. If he was to retain Megan's friendship, and he wanted to, badly; even more than he wanted to make love to her again, which he did; then he'd have to stop running from his feelings and stand his ground. Honestly. There was no room in his life any longer for cowardly self-protection.

Recognising the undisguised self-loathing in Jon's voice, Megan nearly forgave him on the spot, only the reference to other girls he'd made love to, girls who'd undoubtedly been more satisfying in bed than her untutored self, stiffened her spine. Hanging grimly onto the tattered shreds of her anger, she snapped at him.

"I wasn't crying. Or hurting in any way at all after the first little pang, emotionally or physically. Not until you dumped me flat and took off into the night, spoiling everything." She hadn't meant to say all of that; the words had slipped past her guard. Megan compressed her lips, angry at giving so much of herself away.

"You had tears streaming down your face, Megan. Straight after we made love. I saw them Megan. You don't need to cover up your pain, you know," he added gently, only to be repulsed by her angry repudiation.

"Those weren't proper tears! I wasn't crying. Not real crying. It was just the result of emotional overload. Haven't you ever heard of people crying when they're happy?"

Damn. She'd given herself away again.

She should just learn to keep her mouth shut. Then her foot wouldn't be stuck in there all the time, choking her.

Jamming her dark glasses on again, Megan crossed her arms over her chest and slumped back in her corner, staring out the window, making it abundantly plain she'd said all she intended to on the subject.

Happy tears!

Megan had been happy? Happy until he'd ruined it for her. Appalled, Jon finally understood the true nature of his crime in Megan's eyes. He'd been an abysmal fool.

All this pain, for both of them, had been utterly needless. If only he hadn't been such an idiot.

Cursing himself silently, Jon was about to drive on when he recalled the second item on his agenda. Stopping the car again, he turned to the angry woman slouched into the passenger seat.

Exasperated, nearing the limits of her self-control, Megan stared furiously.

"What?" She almost shouted. "Well? What now?"

Daunted by Megan's anger, yet determined to see it through to the end now that he'd started, Jon pressed doggedly on.

"Megan, you were a virgin. I don't suppose you were protected, were you? Making love to you was so completely unplanned, so overwhelming, I forgot to use a condom."

Comprehending his meaning, Megan shook her head.

"No," she informed him, her tone clipped. Acidic.

"I wasn't planning anything either, you know. If it's pregnancy you're worried about, you needn't be. If I am, I'll take care of everything myself. You don't need to worry about it."

"What do you mean, you'll take care of it yourself? How? If you're pregnant, it's my baby too, and I insist on having some say in what happens to it."

Did he just! Megan would see about that! Taking a deep breath, she spoke slowly and clearly.

"I've already considered all this, you know. If I'm pregnant, which I don't believe I can be, then I'll have the baby. No termination. No adoption. I want children. Maybe not like this, but if there's a baby, I'll keep it. And I'll love it. And you needn't get any ridiculous ideas about noble self-sacrifice, either," she added, seeing more words trembling on his lips.

A shotgun wedding wasn't for her. It was love, not duty, she wanted from a husband. From Jon. It took every ounce of self-control to hold back the tears pushing against her tightly closed lids behind the dark glasses.

Swearing savagely under his breath, Jon glared at Megan, well and truly angry now. Both of them fumed, silent again, as he drove on, only the barest of civilities being exchanged for most of the way.

Anger quickly degenerating into pure misery, Jon didn't know what to do next. Where Megan was concerned, it seemed every step he took was wrong.

Remembering how happy they'd both been, dancing at his sister's wedding, he ached to restore that rapport. He liked Megan. He owed her a lot.

She'd been so very good to him, and *this* was how he'd repaid her.

Somehow, he had to discover a way to make it up with her. To restore their friendship. Jon didn't bother to question why this was so important to him. It just was.

Taking her turn at the wheel, Megan replayed their argument in her mind.

Her temper could burn fiercely, but it never lasted long. By now she'd moved beyond her anger of the morning and was looking ahead. Desperately searching for the means to restore their former relationship. Looking for a route to a happy ending. She'd used anger with Jon in a fruitless attempt to wipe away pain; however, she still loved him. At least as deeply as before. Maybe more, now she knew him so much better.

Now she knew what loving him felt like.

If Jon had been truthful, and Megan truly believed he had been, then the whole painful episode had been born from a misunderstanding. He hadn't said he loved her, but surely she couldn't feel so intensely and not have her feelings reciprocated. That would be too cruel of fate. Habitual optimism sneaking back, Megan elected to think positively.

Jon wasn't in love with her. Yet. Maybe he would be soon, as long as she didn't scare him off. His unhappy past pre-disposed him to distrust emotional involvements, and he'd conditioned himself to run from them.

She needed time.

Time to show Jon how much she had to offer. Time to show him how wonderful, how liberating, how fulfilling love could be.

Time for Jon to learn to trust in her love, and not fear it.

Allowing herself to daydream, they were almost home before Megan realised the future was up to her. She would have to be the one to take the first step. And do it quickly, before Jon got out of the car.

Once he escaped to lick his wounds in private, the job of reconciliation would instantly assume mammoth proportions. That much at least she was sure of.

Megan was becoming very familiar with Jonathon Armitage's defensive reactions. Acting decisively, she pulled over, waiting till Jon turned lack-lustre eyes upon her before she spoke.

"Jon, my apologies for the way I spoke to you this morning." At her earnest words, Jon's eyes sharpened, his focus fully on Megan now, instead of being turned inward.

"I was angry and upset then, Jon. I've had time to cool down and see things clearly. You explained your actions, and I believe you." Intuition informed her it was important he know she trusted him to tell the truth; trusted her to believe him.

"We were friends, weren't we Jon? Before all this got in the way."

Jon nodded, and Megan continued.

"I'd like us to go on being friends. Can we? Please?" Although nobody's doormat, bit of pleading at this juncture wouldn't harm her, she thought, and might encourage Jon to treat her kindly.

An enormous weight lifting from his spirit, Jon sat up straighter.

His Megan was so generous. Surely their friendship must be as important to her as it was to him, or she wouldn't have stopped to talk.

"Oh Megan, I've been racking my brains trying to find a way to win back your friendship. I'm glad it's what you want too." Reaching automatically to take her in his arms and seal their bargain with a healing kiss, he found himself being fended off. With a wry smile Megan offered her hand instead, even though she longed to throw herself into his arms.

"No kisses, thank you Jon," she said, wishing she didn't sound such a prissy Victorian Miss. "When you kiss me, things seem to end up going wrong. Let's just be friends. See how it goes, okay?"

Giving herself to Jon last night had been wonderful, but had led to disaster. Now Megan would see what results a bit of denial might achieve; although if she could have foreseen her own frustration she might have chosen a different course of action.

"Friends. Okay Megan." Jon, although piqued by her rejection of his kiss, readily agreed. "But even friends can kiss sometimes, can't they? I've discovered I rather enjoy kissing you, Megan. So be warned." He knew he was on dangerous ground, but he felt light-headed with relief and couldn't help himself.

Fortunately, Megan chose not to take his playful threat amiss, merely turning a Mona Lisa smile on him, while putting the car in gear.

"And Megan?" Jon's hand on her arm stayed their departure. "If there is a baby, promise you'll tell me. Please. No self-sacrifices, I promise, but I really do need to know so I can be there for you."

Megan stared at him, considering his request. Liking him, loving him, for wanting to accept responsibility.

"Okay. Promise."

Megan drove on. For the last few kilometres the atmosphere in the car was pleasant. Light and friendly for the first time all day. At least on the surface.

Edith and Mike were waiting, anxious to hear how the reunion had gone. Megan let Jon do all the talking excusing herself as soon as possible after dinner. She was exhausted, worn out from emotional excesses and a sleepless night. A long hot soak in the tub and an early night held more appeal than company.

Glancing at herself in the mirror while she dried off, Megan paused, stroking her flat tummy, imagining how it would look, sweetly rounded with Jon's baby growing inside her. Suddenly her desire for his baby was as strong as her desire for Jon himself, although so very different in nature.

The timing and circumstances were all wrong, but, oh, wouldn't it be so wonderful if she was pregnant. She checked her calendar, reluctantly calculating she was safe. Probably. Laughter tinged with hysteria warded off inordinate disappointment.

It was such a happy dream; married to Jon, having his baby. Each of them in love with the other. Heaven on earth.

When her head nestled into the pillow the daydream segued into a sleeping dream in which she relived their lovemaking of the night before.

Only this time with a far more satisfactory ending.

SAVING JONATHON ARMITAGE

13

When Megan wished them all a cheerful, sleepy goodnight, Jon took his leave also; with Trixie, who'd spent the weekend being spoiled by Mike, tucked under his arm. He'd dozed a little while Megan drove, but was exhausted by the stress of the last week, topped off by his miserable, guilt stricken night. Sleeping deeply and dreamlessly, he woke early to lie for a time, considering his changed circumstances.

He'd reconciled with his family; something he'd never dared contemplate. Returning to Sydney to be near them was, for the first time in ten years, a feasible option.

Strangely, now he possessed real choices, choices no-one would argue against, he was reluctant to rush away from Oxley Crossing. In the years of wandering from city to city, he'd never felt the sense of home this place had so rapidly instilled in him.

He almost felt as if he belonged in The Crossing.

The difference lay in the people, Jon realised. People in Oxley Crossing had gone out of their way to make him welcome. To help him. They were friendlier, more involved in each other's lives, more of a close-knit community than those he'd mixed with in the cities. Reaching out to him, they'd offered him a genuine place of his own amongst them.

Did he want to belong in Oxley Crossing?

As little as two weeks ago the answer would have been an unequivocal negative. Today, he mulled the question over in his mind. Whichever way he looked at it, the answer now was a cautious affirmative.

Having experienced the warmth of believing he might have arrived in his true home, he wasn't prepared to throw it away without a trial. Not even to return to his family. After his long absence, his old home, though warmly familiar, hadn't felt like home any longer.

His thoughts rambling on, Jon reviewed people he'd met in The Crossing. People who'd quickly become such important influences in his life.

Mike Patterson, his boss, who was willing to take a chance on him; offering friendship, a place to live, and a secure business opportunity to carry him into the future.

Edith Turner who'd taken him under her wing, mothering him and helping him find his feet.

Potentially enduring friends like Alan Morgan, the Morrises and O'Haras. Alan's young daughters had a special niche of their own in his lonely heart.

Even Angie Wilson.

Grinning, Jon recalled how they'd each used the other for their own ends, yet still managed to become firm friends. He'd always have a soft spot for Angie, although she failed to arouse any more tender feelings.

And then there was Megan Patterson.

Megan, who'd given of herself so generously, in so many ways.

Megan, who might, even now, be carrying his baby. An image of Megan growing big with his child led to a dryness in his mouth and a tightness in his groin.

His conscience demanded he do something about Megan, but what?

He'd desired other women, but none of them, not even Cheryl whom he'd planned to marry, had got so deeply under his skin. He didn't love Megan. He didn't! He didn't believe in all that mushy stuff. He did like her a lot, though, as well as want her. It must be that damned energy flow he almost took for granted now. He hardly thought of it, but, forehead creasing into its habitual frown, he had to admit, it certainly enhanced whatever they had going for them.

Megan Patterson was at the centre of everything Oxley Crossing had come to mean to him.

The frown deepened into a scowl until, like the cartoonists' light bulb, a simple solution, one that covered all aspects of his problem, lit up his mind.

He should marry Megan!

"God, I must be mad!" He muttered, appalled at the very idea of marriage. To anyone.

He couldn't have changed so very much as all that! Besides, Megan didn't want to marry him, did she? Wasn't that what she really meant when she'd told him not to even think of acting out of misguided noble self-sacrifice? Shrugging aside the whole troublesome idea he got up abruptly and headed for the shower.

Unfortunately for his peace of mind, the idea refused to stay shelved. Over breakfast he gave in to the nagging demands of his conscience and considered the matter calmly and rationally.

Should he, Jonathon Armitage, marry Megan Patterson? Or not?

He thought it over a while longer, the idea of marriage gradually growing on him. It was a risk, but when he weighed the pros and cons, this time the pros came out on top. Besides, everything truly worthwhile in life carried an inherent risk, didn't it? He could accept Mike's offer if he married Megan, and go on living in The Crossing for as long as he liked. Everyone would be happy; all bases covered. But could he do it?

The longer he thought it over, the more appeal the idea held for him. Staying in The Crossing, which it seemed he wanted to do, he'd be more comfortable with a woman of his own.

With their chemistry, Megan was the obvious choice.

Children too. He'd envied Alan his two girls, so why not have kids of his own?

Believing he'd never marry, fatherhood was something Jon had never sought. Now it was beginning to look quite appealing. Just as well, if Megan did turn out to be pregnant. If she was, she'd soon learn he didn't consider marriage to her to be a sacrifice.

He was sure he wasn't being unreasonably vain in assuming Megan would welcome him as a lover - a husband. His mind still shied away from saying the word. She liked him, most of the time, and his body reminded him of her passionate response to his lovemaking Saturday night.

When he persuaded his Megan to marry him their marriage would be no cold, dutiful arrangement.

Brimful of plans, Jon pulled himself up short. He might be sure of himself at last, but he couldn't simply walk up to Megan and say, 'Guess what, Megan? I've decided we ought to get married.' Not after the miserable fiasco he'd made of Saturday night. Megan was barely talking to him. She didn't trust him; and he couldn't honestly blame her.

A little finesse was required. He'd have to woo his lady before he won her. The challenge of winning Megan excited Jon, overcoming the nervousness caused by even thinking about marriage, and brought a wicked sparkle to his eyes as he set about planning the exercise. From things she'd said, he didn't think there'd been too much romance in Megan's life.

"That's about to change," he confided in Trixie. "From now on there will be."

He'd court Megan romantically, with flowers and sweet words. Lots of attention. He'd sweep her off her feet. And if she landed in his bed, he'd consider it a bonus. In fact, didn't he owe it to her to chase away Saturday's bad memories, replacing them with ones sweeter and more satisfying?

First things first though. As an opening gambit Jon raided the rose garden. Waiting till he saw Mike leave the house, he nipped in to catch Megan alone.

He needed to see Mike to tell him he was accepting the job he'd been offered, but that could wait. Megan came first. Lacking ribbons and wrappings, Jon took his fresh, dewy armful of flowers across, straight from the garden, catching Megan at the breakfast table.

Flowers! Jonathon Armitage was at her door bearing flowers. Megan's heart raced. How sweet of him. She took them from him, smiling her delight.

"It must seem a bit cheeky, bringing you your father's flowers, Megan. Since there's no florist in The Crossing, this was the best I could do." He smiled, his eyes making promises Megan had never received from this man before. Her heart thumped in her chest, and she almost missed his next words.

"They're to say thank you for standing by me and being my friend, Megan. And thank you also for forgiving my stupidity."

Standing the roses in the sink to be dealt with later, a bemused Megan placed both palms on Jon's shoulders and reached up to kiss his cheek; only to have him pull her close, turning his head so her kiss landed on his mouth.

The intended peck was suddenly so much more.

Megan rapidly lost the ability to think lucidly. Her senses were swimming, flooded with the clean, minty taste of Jon's mouth invading hers and the smell of citrus scented after shave lotion mingling with the perfume of roses. Her body remembered the muscular weight of Jon's pressed against it.

Passion threatening to escalate out of control, she felt Jon's hand part the thin robe which was all she was wearing, and gently caress her bare breast.

Mustering the tattered shreds of her self-control, Megan forced herself to push hard against Jon's chest. Turning away from the temptation of masculine lips, she stepped back.

One step, two; grateful to Jon for releasing her.

Elated that his passion matched her own.

Annoyed with herself for making it so easy for him to take advantage. Playing for time, she turned her back and retied her robe. Securely. Shaking her head, she dared to look him in his unrepentant eyes.

"Oh Jon. Talk about inches and miles. You're the absolute limit. I thought we'd only agreed to be friends?"

A new and unfamiliar sexy grin adorning his face, Jon gazed back at her, eyes glinting dangerously.

"True. But Megan, when you're close to me, it's hard to hold back. One taste of your sweetness and I'm greedy for more."

Eyes narrowing, Megan studied Jon suspiciously. Since when had he changed his tune? She'd have found it more believable if he'd tried to evade entanglement. Why was he putting on a Don Juan impersonation? She loved Jon, but she wasn't blind to his faults. The man was up to something, but would his scheming prove good or bad for her?

"How about a ride on the Harley after work?" Jon's still wicked smile suggested he was offering more than a simple ride. "We could watch the sunset from One Tree Hill. According to Marge's brochure, it shouldn't be missed."

Megan hesitated, wanting to accept; still wary, trying to understand Jon's volte face.

"Please come Meggie. It'll be fun."

"Okay, I'll come." Megan replied with a casual air. She wasn't prepared to forego a date with her man, however much her instincts warned her it would be bad strategy to fall into his arms too eagerly.

Satisfied with his progress so far, Jon left Megan to get ready for work, a process delayed while she found a vase for her roses.

~~~~~

"What's all this then?" Megan stared at the crackers, pate and canned drinks Jon was unpacking from a cooler bag.

"This?" Jon's expression was unbelievably innocent. "Just a snack. We've got a while yet to sunset. I've brought straight Pepsi or rum mixer. Which do you prefer?"

The simple ride to watch the sunset appeared to be part of a broader plan. Megan resolved to be on her guard. This new Jonathon Armitage was an unknown quantity.

"Pepsi, please. I'm impressed, Jon. I wasn't expecting all this." Megan scooped pate onto a cracker, rearranging the food between them on the rug. She turned so she could see Jon's face while they talked.

"Dad tells me you're taking the job at the garage. I'm glad, but what happened to your plans to move on? I imagined you'd be off to Sydney to be with your family as soon as you could."

"'I'd intended to tell you myself, this morning. Got distracted and forgot." Jon looked as if he'd rather be distracted again than talk about himself.

Megan munched on another cracker, waiting. She had a vested interest in the answer, and this time she wasn't leaving it to someone else to ask the questions. Jon shrugged, looking away for endless seconds. Finally, he turned back to face Megan.

"Carolyn's letter, and meeting them all on the weekend ... I discovered things I'd believed to be true, weren't. Not when viewed from another person's perspective."

He stared off into space for a moment, choosing his words.

"I'd never actually thought it all through before, just blocked everything out. I've done a lot of thinking the last couple of days. Trying to sort myself out. Gordon went through a rough time with Pam, only he didn't let a bad experience sour him the way I did. Mike accused me of running from my problems, and he was right."

Jon looked miserable. His plans for Megan required honesty between them, so he couldn't afford to baulk at the first hurdle. Taking a deep breath, he moistened his dry mouth with a sip of Pepsi and forced himself to continue.

"Even though they asked me to, I don't really want to return to Sydney. I've discovered I like it here in The Crossing. I believe Mike was right. It's time I stopped running. Time I looked forward instead of back. The Crossing's as good a place as any for that, and better than most."

Moist eyed, Megan reached over and squeezed his hand. Jon laced his fingers through hers, returning the sympathetic squeeze.

"Your support has helped a lot, Meggie. I'd still be running if it wasn't for you."

Too restless to sit still, Jon stood, pulling Megan up with him.

"Let's walk. We'll have a better view of the sunset from the end of the ridge." He was done with introspection. Action was more his style.

Hand in hand they strolled along the path to the viewing platform. Standing close together, eyes on the fiery red and gold blaze fading into sultry pinks and purples, Jon wrapped both arms around Megan, cradling her close in front of him, chin resting on her head. As if Megan's sigh of pleasure was his signal, he dipped his head, nuzzling the soft skin behind her ear; laying a trail of delicious, open mouthed kisses down the length of her neck. His hands stroked wicked caresses over her breasts, circling, teasing.

Impatient, eager for two-way intimacy, Megan diced with danger, turning within the circle of Jon's arms. Threading her fingers through his hair, she tugged his head lower, meeting hot, ready lips with her own. Wildfire coursing through her veins turned Megan's bones to jelly. She loved this man. Wanted him with a fierce passion. Yet, when Jon began working on the buttons of her blouse, she tore her lips from his, dropping her forehead to rest against the base of his throat.

"No. No more Jon." Too weak to stand alone she leaned against him a few seconds longer.

"Meggie?" Jon rasped. "Let me show you how good we can be together. You know you want me as much as I want you."

"I do know, Jon. Just ... not now. Please? You said it before. Your whole world has been turned topsy-turvy. So has mine. You need time to sort yourself out. I need time too. To be sure of where I'm going. At least for now, I'd rather take it slowly."

Megan wasn't a woman for the short term.

She knew she'd already comprised her own firm policy on Saturday night, but this was now. Jon was staying till he got himself sorted, but the speed he was progressing, that would likely be sooner, rather than later. Caution warred with desire resulting in confusion.

If an affair was all he had to offer, she might yet take him up on it, but until she saw her way clear, one way or the other, she'd contain her impatience and wait.

Jon huffed out a huge sigh, his breath ruffling the top of her hair. Removing his hands from where they'd stilled on her sweetly rounded breasts, he wrapped them round Megan's back in a firm hug. Her hair muffled his voice, so she barely heard his whispered words.

"And I'd rather take you, Megan Patterson. Slow or fast. Anywhere, any time."

A fiery blush heating her cheeks, Megan pushed herself upright, stepping out of the warmth of Jon's embrace. She peered into his face. A face as grim and forbidding as she'd ever seen it.

"I'm not playing fair, am I? Egging you on, then saying no. Jon, I'm not being a deliberate tease. I'm truly not ready. I'm sorry."

"It's okay. My brain tells me I won't die of frustration but my body hasn't got the message yet." His dark expression easing, Jon slung an arm round Megan's shoulder and walked her back to the rug.

"Damn!"

He hadn't allowed himself to get angry with Megan.

The bull-ants feasting on pate and crackers weren't so lucky. Tossing the food into the bin, Jon shook the rug free of invaders. At the sound of Megan's nervous giggle, he stiffened, then saw the funny side and laughed along with her.

His plans for a romantic seduction had been doomed from the start, but, he reminded himself, there was always tomorrow. When Megan invited him to dinner, he felt confidence flooding back.

Tonight had been no more than the opening skirmish in 'Operation Megan.'

14

Over the next few days, Megan spent every evening with Jon, and most of her lunch breaks as well. He gave her the time she'd asked for, while being attentive enough to leave her aching with frustration when they parted, and, for the first time, she learned how it felt to be a desirable, sought-after woman.

In Jon's arms she was so happy she felt beautiful. Was beautiful.

Jon was assiduous in his pursuit, cornering her for stolen kisses, taking her riding on the Harley and down to the Victoria for a drink and a lesson in the game of pool; where he left her in no doubt he'd rather be giving her a lesson in the game of love. Each evening he sought her out.

Mike, intent on his own courtship, usually left them to their own devices. The rose arbour in the back garden became their favourite rendezvous.

While Megan stuck to her decision to wait till she was sure of Jon's true feelings, her body was fast developing a mind of its own. Her resistance became gossamer-fragile, but was not yet at breaking point.

Friday morning Megan woke late to be confronted by the unmistakable evidence that she was definitely not pregnant. She'd have to tell Jon as soon as possible, she supposed, only she was running late and there was no time right away. Lunchtime would be soon enough.

In the middle of dressing, a chilling possibility occurred to her. Slumping down on the edge of her bed, head sunk in her hands, she examined the evidence.

What if all Jon's lovely attention this week had been due to the baby she wasn't having?

Thinking back, she recalled the way he'd several times rubbed her tummy, a strange, contemplative expression on his face. Once he'd wondered aloud if their baby was a boy or girl; as if its existence were an established fact. Certain of her dates, she'd laughingly dismissed the possibility, but what if Jon truly believed in it, in spite of her denials?

How would he react to the news there was no baby?

He hadn't shown any interest in a relationship with her before, so would he drop her now, relieved to be free of a responsibility he'd been prepared to assume out of a sense of duty?

Megan was fiercely glad she'd resisted his blandishments all week. It would make disentanglement so much easier, for both of them, she told herself with bleak realism.

Depressed by what she rapidly convinced herself was the most likely truth, Megan finished dressing and dragged herself downstairs to work.

Hadn't she always known a man like Jonathon Armitage, who could have any woman he chose, would have little lasting interest in a plain, ordinary woman like herself? She'd jealously observed the speculatively admiring looks he drew from women of all ages.

Why had she given in to the delusion of interpreting a lusty man's reaction to an available woman as an attraction that could evolve into genuine love?

Shamelessly, she'd thrown herself at him.

Then, imagining a baby was involved; his baby, he'd decided to do the honourable thing and had had the good manners to sugar coat it for her.

This theory even explained the mysterious sense of calculation that had aroused her suspicions a few days earlier.

Plummeted defencelessly into the depths of despair, Megan lost the glowing radiance happiness had bestowed upon her.

Now, abandoning hope, she looked plain and dreary; in her own eyes at least. Warding off threatening tears by sheer will power, she kept as busy as possible while the clock inched its way to lunchtime. Her moment of truth.

Arriving too early in the rose arbour, she slumped, hugging her pain to herself, on the seat she'd grown accustomed to sharing with Jon.

Whistling a lively ditty, Trixie gambolling at his heels as usual, Jon stopped short at the sight of Megan's woebegone face.

What on earth had cast his happy, cheerful Megan into the dumps? A guilty review of his own recent actions assured him *he* couldn't possibly be responsible; there had to be another, unknown, cause. Relieved to be innocent, Jon slipped onto the seat beside her, gathering her into comforting arms.

"What is it Meggie? What's wrong? However bad it is, you can count on me."

She could, could she? Sadly, Megan didn't think so. Raising her eyes to flick a glance at Jon's concerned face, she blurted out her news.

"I'm not pregnant Jon! There's not going to be any baby! Isn't that good news?"

Shivering, she fought against incipient tears. Men hated tears. She'd spare Jon that ordeal. Besides, it would only embarrass her to let Jon see her crying over him.

No baby! It *should* be good news, but Jon was shocked at the depth of his disappointment. He'd begun taking fatherhood for granted; part of the package deal he'd decided on. He'd even gone so far as to consider names. But this was no time to wallow in selfish, maudlin sentimentality. Megan needed him.

It was up to him to give her all the comfort he was capable of. She must have really wanted this baby, more than she'd let on; otherwise, why the devastation? He vowed to be extra specially tender and caring. Once Megan was over her disappointment, he'd step up the pace of his campaign; make her his as soon as possible. They had all the rest of their lives for babies.

Jon was kindness personified, tearing at Megan's heart.

The man was letting her down gently, not tossing her aside abruptly as she'd half expected. Every new facet of his personality she uncovered strengthened her yearning for him.

If only he loved her back.

Contrary to Megan's gloomy expectations, Jon spent as much time with her as during the previous week. Was as tender and romantic as before.

Torn between the sweetness of his attentions and the pain of their inevitable parting, which she still felt certain was imminent, Megan fell prey to sleeplessness and depression. A depression she strove desperately to disguise. It was only another week till her father's wedding. Her misery couldn't be permitted to mar this special time for Mike and Eddie.

Throwing herself into the last-minute flurry of preparations for the big day, as well as organising a bridal shower for Edith and getting her house ready to accommodate visiting wedding guests, Megan kept herself too busy to dwell on her own problems. Time enough for that later, when all the fuss died down and she was alone.

By her most recent calculations, that would also be when Jon phased himself out of her life. He was too kind to go upsetting her now, spoiling her enjoyment of the wedding.

As the only bridesmaid, and Mike's daughter, she absolutely had to present a happy face. Jon really wasn't the cold, care-for-nobody lone wolf she'd first thought him, so of course he'd wait till after the wedding to make the break.

With the wedding so close, Jon knew Megan had little time to spare for him, but that was okay; he could wait.

When he let himself dwell on the responsibilities of marriage, he was almost happy to put it off. Except that he'd made up his mind and intended to stick to his decision. In a few days, there'd be plenty of time for them.

Megan appeared to be over her disappointment, and so was he. When he thought about it, he acknowledged it was for the best. They had years ahead of them for babies, and Megan didn't deserve to be the subject of the inevitable gossip a baby would have generated. He'd taken a precautionary shopping trip; next time he made love to his woman there'd be no need to fear adverse consequences.

~~~~~

Eddie and Mike's wedding was as near perfection as any bride could wish. Even the weather co-operated, bright and sunny with a cooling breeze.

The bride, aglow with love and excitement, looked so much younger and prettier than she actually was.

Her floating, cream chiffon dress, reminiscent of an old-fashioned tea gown, swirled around slim calves. A ribbon and roses fascinator anchored to the front of her hair and a bouquet of Pierre de Ronsard roses from her own garden completed the image of a picture-perfect mature bride.

Edith had loved her Stan, but he'd been dead a long time. Now she revelled in her second chance at love and marriage with Mike, who'd been her good friend for so long.

There he stood, proud and happy in his new suit, waiting for her at the altar; Jack O'Hara his best man once again, second time around.

The solemnity of the moment, as the two middle-aged lovers exchanged their vows had Jon feeling slightly choked up. The next wedding he attended would probably be his own. Momentarily daunted by the prospect, he turned his eyes to Megan, seeking reassurance that he really was doing the right thing.

She was a delight in her shell pink gown sprigged with tiny flowers, the style complementing the bride's. A wreath of baby-pink miniature roses drew attention to her lovely dark-rimmed blue eyes shaded by twin fans of long, curling lashes.

Pride filled Jon's heart, chasing out the shadows of his momentary fear.

Megan Patterson was *his* woman; his lovely, beguiling woman. His imagination drifted into the future, to the excitement of his anticipated wedding night with Megan. Embarrassed by his body's instant response to his erotic imaginings, Jon quickly steered his thoughts into safer channels.

After the bridal couple departed, enroute for a honeymoon on Daydream Island on the Great Barrier Reef, Jon claimed Megan for the last dance.

Dancing with his Megan, he discovered, was rapidly becoming addictive; she fitted so perfectly in his arms. He drew her closer, breathing in the intoxicating mixture of her perfume blending with the scent of the fresh roses in her hair.

It was such a pity she had a houseful of guests. Tonight would have been the perfect occasion to erase those bad memories in the most pleasurable manner.

~~~~~

Several nights later, Jon morosely stared through his window, watching lights clicking on and off in Megan's house as she locked up and prepared for bed.

'Operation Megan' was foundering; and Jon couldn't figure out why.

He'd romanced her, demonstrated his desire for her, and shown her his sincere need to make her part of his life. He'd even confided his deepest feelings, so why did Megan continue to resist?

Why hadn't she fallen into his arms by now?

If he were honest with himself, Jon admitted, Megan's resistance now was stronger, more determined, than in the beginning.

Tonight he'd come dangerously close to losing his temper when Megan gently repulsed him yet again, putting him out of her house politely but firmly; a flash of her own temper showing when he demurred.

He wanted her so badly he sometimes felt he was going crazy. Their one night together had proved to him that Megan returned his desire, so why wasn't his plan working?

Obviously, he was doing something wrong, but what?

Jon still hadn't reached any conclusions by the time he crawled, frustrated and lonely, into his own cold, empty bed.

Until he identified the problem, how could he devise a solution?

~~~~~

So wrapped in gloomy thoughts the next morning that even Trixie's antics failed to bring more than a fleeting half smile to his face, Jon was jolted abruptly into full awareness of his surroundings.

He found himself being confronted by Jack O'Hara, glaring at him over the mug of coffee he thrust out aggressively. Startled, he looked into the older man's gruff, determined face.

"Spending a lot of time chasing after our Meggie, aren't you?" Jack considered himself in loco parentis during Mike's absence, and took the responsibility seriously.

"I sure hope you mean well by her, son. She's kinda special to some of us. We wouldn't like to see her hurt by some young fella who's just amusing himself."

Tugging his moustache in embarrassment, Jack turned abruptly and stomped off leaving Jon staring after him, mouth opened as if to protest the attack.

'Is that what he thinks? More to the point, is that what Megan thinks?'

Brushing aside his fleeting annoyance with Jack's interference, Jon sat down to think the matter through. Knowing he fully intended to marry his lady once he'd won her, he hadn't looked at the situation from this angle before. Sipping his coffee, he took his time.

For all her generous spirit, Jack's intervention reminded Jon his Megan had been strictly brought up and was more than a little bit straight laced. He'd set out to seduce her for the sheer fun of it, for both of them, intending to follow seduction with an honourable proposal.

Should he reverse his strategy and take the old-fashioned approach? Megan wasn't a sexually modern woman, happy to fall into bed with the man of the moment.

By the time his coffee mug was empty, Jon had conceived a new strategy. The time for playing games was over. It was time to get serious; to tell Megan what he really wanted. Riskier perhaps, but they'd both know where they stood with no room for ambiguities. No room for mistakes.

Flowers and champagne to soften her up, a straight forward proposal, and hopefully he'd have his Megan falling into his arms at last.

Jon's fantasies skidded to an abrupt halt. Damn! He'd have to wait. Megan was visiting a client tonight. A farmer, too busy harvesting to get into town. They were old friends and so Megan had agreed to share a family dinner, and discuss business later.

Tomorrow then.

With more time to plan, Jon became more ambitious. A romantic dinner for two. At home, where he'd have Megan all to himself. Champagne still, since he anticipated a reason for celebration.

Whistling cheerfully, Jon rinsed his mug and took it back to the coffee machine out front, calling out to Jack as he passed.

"It's okay, you know, Jack. You needn't worry about Megan. My intentions are completely honourable. You'll see."

Jack's dropped jaw and stunned gaze had Jon grinning broadly as he returned to the car he was working on, confidence fully restored. Positive he had got it right this time.

All that remained was for Megan to say 'Yes'.

~~~~~

Waking early the following morning, considerably earlier than usual, Megan rolled over with a groan and tried to recapture sleep. No good. Once she woke, she usually stayed awake.

Mentally listing all the domestic chores she'd been putting off recently, she decided she may as well tackle some of them before breakfast. Household tasks tended to be low on her list of favourite occupations, but until she could afford a housekeeper, she had to do them herself or live in squalor; and her mother had taught her better than that.

Drowsily, she glanced next door from the bathroom window. It was too early to catch a glimpse of Jon, but out of habit, she paused to look anyway.

Icy-skinned, feet rooted to the floor and heart palpitating wildly after missing a beat, Megan stared, afraid she might be about to faint.

What was Angie Wilson doing, leaving Jon's flat at this hour?

Oh, she could imagine why of course; her mind was quick to provide a selection of lurid images. While she watched, unable to turn away, Jon, clad only in the white boxer shorts she remembered with a pang, hair still rumpled from bed, stepped into view.

Angie threw her arms around him, hugging him enthusiastically, before running down the steps and off through the garden. Jon stepped back inside and shut the door. Megan slumped to the floor, shivering convulsively as she leaned against the side of the tub.

Her worst fears had suddenly manifested themselves, striking her numb; too sick at heart for mere tears.

Not only did Jon not love her; he'd turned to Angie again when Megan refused him the shallow relationship he sought. If she hadn't seen them together this morning, she'd have made an even bigger fool of herself than she already had.

She and Jon had come close to having a fight the last time they'd seen each other. Thinking perhaps she was being silly and over-prudish, Megan had decided to let Jon have his way next time. She wanted him, too, and it was so very hard to keep saying 'No'. He hadn't backed off after the wedding as she'd expected, so she'd thought perhaps his intentions were serious. Tentatively, she'd dared to hope again. She'd hoped true love might grow out of physical love. No longer though.

Those fragile hopes had been dashed. Completely.

Megan wished she'd never met Jonathon Armitage. Never fallen in love with him. All it had brought her was heartache after heartache. Heartache she'd rather live without.

'But only heroines in books can afford the luxury of giving in to their broken hearts,' she sniffled. *'In real life a girl has to pick herself up, put the pieces back together somehow, and carry on with her life.'*

By concentrating fiercely on each small step, Megan pulled herself together to face the demands of her busy day. Immersing herself in work, avoiding as many people as possible, she made it to her last appointment of the day without breaking down.

~~~~~

Jon, his immediate schemes uppermost in his mind, finished work early to allow himself time to set the scene. Having missed Megan at lunchtime for the second day in a row, he filled his arms with as many roses as Mike's recently depleted garden could yield, and set out in search of her.

She ought to be finishing up in her office, so he'd catch up with her there and issue his dinner invitation before she had time to busy herself elsewhere.

Checking momentarily, he thought uneasily of the last two lunch breaks when Megan failed to join him. Had she really been too busy, or had she been avoiding him? Well, he thought, an uncharacteristic pugnacious tilt to his chin, he was about to settle any doubts Megan might have regarding his intentions. Then she'd have no reason to avoid him again, if that was really what she'd been doing.

In the foyer he met Megan's last client of the day, Elizabeth Tan, on her way out.

"Ooh, what lovely roses. Are they for Megan?" she trilled, turning back to her friend. "You lucky girl, Megan. No-one ever brings me lovely flowers like these."

At the sight of Jon, smiling confidently at her over the top of an armful of roses, Megan was seized by a blazing fury.

How dare the rat bring flowers to her, after spending the night with Angie Wilson!

Thrown out a little by Elizabeth's interruption and knowing smile, Jon came straight to the point, without noticing they were not yet alone. Without noticing Megan's dangerous expression. Proffering the roses, he cheerfully issued his invitation.

"I've come to ask you to have dinner with me tonight, Meggie."

About to blast the damned man out of her office, Megan became aware of Elizabeth, hovering on the doorstep to hear her reply. With a massive effort, she curbed her temper.

"Dinner too," cooed Elizabeth. "This man's a real prize, Megan. Hang onto him, girl."

Winking slyly, she finally left them alone and Jon thankfully closed the door behind her.

There was no malice in Elizabeth's interest; quite the reverse in fact. Pity she'd butted in, though, Jon thought, eyeing Megan's outraged expression. Directing his attention to Megan again, he smiled sympathetically.

"How about it then, Meggie? Will you have dinner with me?" Jon smiled again, his warmest, most heart melting smile, wondering why Megan didn't say something, or take the roses from him even. She just stood there by her desk, as if frozen to the spot. Staring at him, lost in thought.

After taking a long moment to think before she blurted out something irrevocable, Megan stepped forward with a cool smile and finally accepted the flowers.

"Elizabeth's right. These roses are lovely. Thank you, Jon, and yes, I will come to dinner." Burying her face in the blooms, she avoided looking at Jon.

Megan was utterly confused. Here was Jon, acting as if his conscience was quite clear. As if *she* were the only woman he was interested in.

As if he was inviting her to more than a simple meal.

They'd shared meals before, without all this fuss over the invitation. Megan was still angry, still hurting, only Elizabeth's intervention had given her a moment's grace to consider her options.

In case there *was* some innocent explanation for what she'd seen, she'd hold her temper till she had her facts straight.

If she hadn't made a mistake, *then* she'd kill him. Slowly and painfully. Her eyes glittered as she imagined slicing him into tiny pieces with a blunt knife. With the light behind her, casting her face into shadow, Jon remained unaware of the danger signs.

In ignorance of Megan's true mood, he was still standing there, smiling expectantly at her. Unsure what to do next in view of what he interpreted as a sadly lacklustre response, Jon pressed a quick kiss to her brow, the only part of her face readily accessible behind the flowers.

"That's great then. I'll see you at seven Meggie. Now I'd better get started in the kitchen." With another beaming smile, he slipped out the door.

Megan hadn't been exactly rapturous, but then, maybe Elizabeth's remarks had inhibited her. Jon shrugged, refusing to admit any doubts.

~~~~~

About to don one of her prettier dresses, Megan shoved it back in the closet. She absolutely refused to dress up for that two-timing polecat. No way. Defiantly, she pulled on comfortable old faded jeans and a plain country-style white blouse with blue piping, completing the casual look with well-worn boots and a hand-tooled leather belt.

Although Megan was in no mood to appreciate it, the outfit suited her, emphasising her tiny waist; the butter-soft denim lovingly moulding her shapely bottom. Half-way down the stairs, she turned and ran back up to apply a light make-up and spray on some of her favourite perfume.

Not for Jon. For herself.

With a hard, almost bitter smile at her reflection, she set off again, armoured to face whatever disaster awaited her next door.

Impatience urged Megan to demand outright an explanation for Angie's presence. Afraid of being lied to, she elected to wait and see, because one thing she was absolutely certain of.

Jonathon Armitage was up to something.

He welcomed her ceremoniously, plying her with champagne.

Romantic music played softly, and the table was set with a good linen tablecloth and crystal glasses she was sure belonged to Judy O'Hara. Complete with a floral centrepiece, it looked set for a celebration.

Celebration! Megan pretended her disgusted snort was merely a muffled sneeze.

Thoroughly confused, but still suspicious of Jon's motives, she resolved not to let the champagne go to her head since it was beginning to look as if she'd better keep her wits about her. Especially as Jon was on top of his form, whistling to the background music as he put the finishing touches to the meal.

If she hadn't seen Angie with her own eyes, Megan would have been putty in his hands.

Disregarding his fleeting disappointment that Megan hadn't bothered to dress up for him, Jon, himself clad in the best his severely limited wardrobe had to offer, greeted her warmly, sliding his hands down to cup her denim-clad bottom; drawing her into his arms. His Megan wore jeans well, as he'd observed on a number of occasions, and he'd given her no warning this was to be a special evening. Disconcerted, he gave a mental shrug when she pushed herself determinedly out of his embrace.

Pouring the champagne, he warned himself to go easy on the bubbly. This date was too important to risk a slip-up. He needed a clear head in case Megan did something unpredictable; especially as she seemed to be in a strange mood today. He might need to think fast.

Jon's confidence faltered briefly when he remembered that once before he'd failed to get his bride to the altar. Hastily, he reassured himself. Cheryl had been very different to Megan. Really, she'd done him a favour, dumping him. His sweet Megan Patterson, with her old-fashioned values regarding marriage and family, would suit him so much better.

Whistling to himself, Jon checked the oven. Almost ready. His culinary repertoire wasn't wide, but what it did include, he'd learned to cook well. He was confidant Megan would enjoy his lasagne and garlic bread. The fresh garden salad waiting in the fridge only needed to have the dressing tossed through it before he put it on the table. Desserts not being his forte, he'd bought a flan filled with fruit and custard from the bakery, once again running the gauntlet of Elizabeth's teasing.

By now, most of Oxley Crossing probably knew he was entertaining Megan with a romantic dinner in his flat.

Speculation would undoubtedly be running high. Unfazed, Jon looked forward to sharing the news of their engagement with their friends. Pulling his thoughts up sharply, he reminded himself to keep his mind on the job, or he'd mess it all up. Yet again. Although never once did he seriously consider Megan might refuse him.

His Megan was not the girl to surrender herself to him as willingly, as passionately, as she had that night in Sydney unless she had very strong feelings for him. He'd convinced himself she was only waiting for him to make a proper commitment to her before she fell into his eagerly waiting arms once more.

Desire as strong as his just had to be reciprocal.

Placing the food on the table he'd taken such pains over, Jon ushered Megan to her chair, topping up her glass before taking his seat opposite. Keeping the conversation light, he introduced topics he knew Megan to be interested in, working hard to relax her; to lull her into a receptive mood.

~~~~~

Love for Jonathon Armitage was tearing Megan apart.

When Jon looked at her, seducing her with his eyes as he was now, she felt her shield of anger dissolving; her resolution wavering.

Conversation faltered as Jon's eyes caressed her from across the table, their heat lingering on lips that ached for his; sliding over her delicately flushed cheeks and the sweet hollow at the base of her throat then dipping lower, plunging hotly into the opening at the top of her blouse which permitted a glimpse of the shadowed valley between her breasts.

Megan's breath caught in her throat.

Desire coursing through her she was unable to swallow another bite. Fists clenched in her lap, she clung desperately to her sanity. However, when her eyes locked hungrily on Jon's, she found it impossible to look away. A leaden ball of tension was building low down in her belly; her breasts tingled, straining against confining fabric.

This was more like it, Jon exulted. Megan was back with him again. Back from whatever faraway place she'd been lost in since she'd arrived. Making no attempt to disguise his desire, he adored her with his eyes. The breath caught in his throat, his mouth dried and his jeans grew taut across his thighs as his body responded to the answering desire he read on Megan's face.

Jon's imagination ran riot, picturing the rapturous lovemaking he was sure would follow Megan's acceptance of his proposal. Last time had been more about him; this time would be all for Megan. He ached to please her; and in so doing, please himself as well.

Breathless, Megan watched Jon come to her. Taking her hands in both of his, he lifted her out of her chair, crushing her to his chest as his lips claimed hers. Melting into his embrace, Megan revelled in his possession of her.

Until a sanity-saving subconscious kicked in, reminding her that this was the same two-timing louse she'd seen farewelling his other woman just that very morning! Hands that had stroked a moment ago now pushed him away. Megan wrenched her mouth free, turning her head to the side, gasping for breath.

Reining in his passion, Jon eased his grip, hands barely clasping Megan's shoulders. Time to slow down.

"Dance with me, Meggie." A command, not a plea. Jon released one hand to turn the music up a little. Kicking a scatter rug out of the way, he swung Megan into a slow waltz, arms binding her to him, their own special brand of electricity tingling through them from every point where their bodies touched.

They danced slowly round the room, moving in a rhythm all their own. Drawing closer and closer in each other's arms.

Grey eyes, shimmering with erotic promises, gazed unblinking into blue.

With a throaty mewl Megan surrendered to the moment, pressing herself as close as humanly possible against Jon's hard body.

'Just a few seconds,' she appeased her inner mentor, *'then I'll face reality again.'* This was one of those magical memories to preserve against the desolate years to come.

Unless maybe, just maybe, she discovered an innocent explanation for what she'd seen. Not that she'd been able to think of one, but oh, how she wished there was. More than anything Megan wanted to trust Jon; to believe he had not betrayed her.

But she needed to *know,* one way or the other. It was imperative she discover the truth. Tonight. Now.

Jon was kissing her again, their lips melding briefly before he leaned back, cupping her face in his hands. Voice deepening with emotion, Jon was speaking urgently. What was he saying? Shaking off her preoccupation, Megan strove to concentrate.

"I want you Meggie. Need you. Meggie, will you marry me?"

Marry! Jon was asking her to marry him!

That was what this elaborate set-up tonight was about!

Jonathon Armitage was asking her, Megan Patterson, to marry him!

Megan's heart soared, elated at this answer to her most heartfelt prayers. Then crashed to earth with a thud.

Jon had said 'want' and 'need'. What about 'love'?

Did Jon love her? Or did he believe friendship and desire were all that was necessary for a successful marriage? She wished she understood how men think. Tonight, her inexperience was a real handicap. And where did Angie fit in? Why had Jon chosen her over Angie?

Answers! Where could she find the answers she so urgently needed? Marriage to Jon was her dearest wish, only how could she accept with so many doubts and questions barring her way?

What was wrong?

An eternity had passed since Jon asked Megan to marry him.

Her expressive face had registered an initial flash of joy when he'd been certain acceptance trembled on her lips, plummeting to the despair with which she gazed at him now. Why wasn't she saying anything? Suddenly afraid of a negative answer, Jon scrambled to avert disaster.

"Have I taken you by surprise, Meggie? If you're not sure, there's no need to answer immediately. Take some time to think it over, if you want." Self-confidence faltering now, all his instincts screamed that if he pushed for an answer tonight, it might be a 'No', and he knew when Megan made up her mind she didn't change it readily. Not without an excellent reason.

Until he identified and resolved her doubts, it was vital that she leave her options open. He needed time to turn the situation around.

"Come on Meggie, let's take a walk while you think it over."

It was the best distraction Jon could come up with on the spur of the moment.

He led Megan over to the door. Her hand clasped firmly in his, Jon urged her down the steps, surprised when she stopped abruptly and sat down, four steps from the bottom.

This had been her 'thinking step' when she was a child living in the flat above the garage with her parents, and old habit had kicked in. Megan's mind was in a whirl. She needed to think, and this was the place to do it. Here, not out walking around town in the dark.

Sliding over against the handrail, Megan made way for Jon as he sank down uncertainly beside her.

He'd been pretty quick telling her to take her time. Had his proposal been an impulsive response to the passion flaring between them, regretted as soon as uttered? Megan didn't think so. Tonight had been planned. Nothing about it had been impulsive, except for her own wild response to Jon's kisses.

After a long moment of silent pondering, Megan threw caution to the winds, offering a counter proposal of her own.

"You know, Jon, you don't need to marry me just to get me to go to bed with you. If that's what this is all about, we can turn around right now and go back upstairs. We can have an affair that lasts as long or as short a time as suits us both. No strings attached."

She was gambling with fate, but Megan was beyond caring. She loved Jon; and if he didn't love her as she wanted to be loved, then she'd take what was left.

Shocked, Jon turned on her, his voice harsh and angry.

"What are you talking about? Damn it all, Megan, I don't want an affair. I asked you to marry me, and the least you can do is take me seriously."

How could she have misjudged him so badly? Surely Megan knew he had more respect for her than that? Her reply stunned him.

"Why? Why do you want to marry me Jon? Just what does your proposal actually mean?" If it was time for plain speaking, she'd ask her questions; and be damned if she didn't like the answers.

"Because ..." Suddenly confused, Jon went on slowly, searching for a truthful answer. "I don't know why, Megan. Not for sure. I just do. Marrying you feels like the right thing for me to do." He looked at her helplessly.

"Try Jon. Please. This is important to me."

"Okay, I'll try." Jon looked at Megan, unhappily aware he'd lost control of the situation and was floundering in unknown territory. He took several deep breaths, gathering his thoughts, then he began, hesitantly at first, more confidently as he got into his stride.

"I really like you Megan. Respect you too. We're friends, and I trust you. I desire you as well. A lot. You know that, but I want a lot more from you than just an affair. I want us to build a life together. Have kids even."

Jon reached for Megan's hands, holding on tightly, as if he was afraid she fly away if he didn't.

"Now that I've decided to stay in The Crossing I want to settle down properly; and that includes marriage. You've helped me to lay my ghosts, Meggie, but I still need your support and understanding. Please say you'll marry me."

This was close, although Megan had a question or two to go before she felt she could safely follow her heart.

"What about Angie Wilson? There was a lot of gossip about the two of you for a while."

There, she'd given him an opening to explain what the other girl meant to him. Why she'd been in his flat last night.

"Angie?' She's just a friend. She's got nothing to do with us."

Jon's surprise sounded genuine. Megan listened closely as he elaborated.

"Angie's in love with Alan Morgan. The two of them are head over heels in love with each other, but they're always fighting over something. If that's what love does to you, then I'm glad I'm not in love."

Glancing up as he finished speaking, Jon was in time to see the shock-wave that shuddered across Megan's face before she managed to hide her feelings behind an impassive mask.

15

Damn! Damn! Damn! He was the biggest fool in creation. Revelation burst upon Jon like fireworks going off in his brain. For all her pragmatism, his Megan was a romantic at heart. It was a declaration of love she'd wanted from him. Almost begged him for. Cruelly, he'd virtually told her to her face that he didn't love her.

He didn't, not in the romantic sense he imagined was what was important to her. But what he did feel was pretty special. Better than being in love, in his opinion.

Love was an emotion he didn't trust, didn't want. People seemed to fall out of love just as violently as they fell into it. He preferred the solid ground of friendship and mutual interests, which he'd already found with Megan, on which to build a marriage.

Not the shifting sands of love.

Common sense dictated his way was more certain to prove lasting. Except that girls liked romance. This love stuff seemed important to them. Surely, if he'd been thinking he could have prevaricated a little, without lying outright. Now he'd really blown his chances with Megan.

Possibly for good. He'd do his best to repair the damage, but it wasn't going to be easy.

Damn his big mouth!

The shrill summons of the telephone cut into Jon's angry thoughts.

Whoever it was had sure picked their moment. Jon didn't know whether to be relieved to be saved by the bell, or annoyed at the interruption. Tempted to ignore it, he was still undecided when Megan urged him sharply to answer it, pain adding an unfamiliar edge to her voice.

"Hurry up Jon. You'd better get that. It might be important."

It was. Sergeant Don Matthews was on the other end, ringing from his mobile phone. There'd been an accident out on Woodcock's Road, a bad one involving two cars. One of the drivers was trapped in his vehicle, and the tow-truck with its winching equipment was urgently required at the scene. Apologetically, Jon explained to Megan what had happened.

"I know we still need to talk, Meggie, but this is more urgent. I'll get back to you as quickly as I can."

"I'll come too." Megan pushed brusquely past him, running for the garage doors. "I've done this sort of thing with Dad lots of times. You'll need my help. Come on, there's no time to waste arguing."

About to protest, Jon shut his mouth. Megan was right, there wasn't time to argue, and maybe she would be useful.

~~~~~

'Well', Megan thought, *'I demanded answers. Now I've got them, haven't I.'*

The problem of Angie was apparently no problem at all, even though she still had no idea why the woman had been at Jon's flat. Momentarily diverted, Megan wondered about Angie and Alan Morgan. By all accounts they'd had a torrid but short-lived affair not long after Angie arrived at the Victoria. Was that back on again? If so, the grapevine had been strangely silent. They must be keeping a very low profile. Perhaps what they had was the real thing.

Megan had come full circle. Back to herself and Jonathon Armitage. Jon wasn't in love with Angie, but he wasn't in love with her, either. She loved him desperately, only she wasn't sure she was strong enough to marry him without being loved in return.

She feared unrequited love might fester, eventually turning to resentment, making them both unhappy.

Doubts still tormented her when they arrived at the sharp bend on Woodcock's Road where a station wagon had collided head-on with a small sedan. The tangled wreckage of the two vehicles, still locked together, lay precariously balanced against a scrubby little gum tree half-way down the steep river bank.

Don Matthews had managed to get a line from the winch on his police four-wheel drive truck down to them, to hold them steady.

Doc Rogers, earlier on the scene than themselves, was attending to one driver on the side of the road.

Thrown clear, he appeared battered and bruised with a nasty gash above his eye, but otherwise was in reasonable condition. It was the elderly man driving the second car who was the problem.

Conscious but dazed, he was trapped by the crumpled metal pressing down on his legs. He couldn't be removed from the wreckage till the station wagon was winched away from where it leaned dangerously against the smaller car. If the station wagon slipped, it would most likely take the other vehicle with it, plunging them both into the river at the foot of the slope. A steep slope, with few trees or boulders to block their descent. The spindly sapling and Don's winch cable were all that was keeping the two vehicles out of the water.

While Don explained to Jonathon what he wanted him to do, Megan got busy readying the equipment. As she'd told Jon, this was something she'd done before with her father and she knew how to make herself useful, helping to operate the heavy-duty winch and fetching and carrying under the men's directions.

Mike had insisted she become familiar with every piece of equipment on the big, modern tow-truck which had been his pride and joy until he handed its operation over to Jon.

Doc Rogers slipped and slithered down the slope to see what injuries the second driver had sustained.

As he scrambled back up to the road, his grim expression warned them the situation was not good. Panting from exertion, he outlined the problem.

"He has a bump on the head and his legs are trapped. As far as I can tell, one of them is crushed and badly broken. He'll need to be handled carefully, and speed is of the essence. There's bound to be serious bleeding, his blood pressure is way down already and still dropping. We must get him out quickly. I think I can rig an IV line through the window, but I really should get inside with him to see what I'm dealing with."

The doctor looked helplessly down at himself. He was a big man, badly out of condition; and the only way into the tiny car was via the window in the jammed front passenger door; the side facing down the slope.

A difficult access for anyone, it would be impossible for the elderly doctor. It would be at least another twenty minutes before the ambulance arrived from Tamworth, and that might be too late for the injured man if he was bleeding as Doc Rogers believed he was.

Taking a deep breath, Megan eyed the three men, all much taller and broader than herself. "I can climb in with him Doc." Her tone defied argument. "Tell me what to do and I'll try. Don, if you and Jon can get the station wagon out of the way, then we can get him out. Let's get started."

The doctor merely nodded, already working out in his mind what he needed to do for his patient. He jogged to his car, hurrying to assemble the necessary items. Don began directing Jon to attach his heavy winch onto the station wagon to move it. His own lighter one would have to do to support the smaller car against being dislodged from its precarious perch. They would put a second cable on it as well, just to be on the safe side, he decided.

"Come on Armitage, get cracking," he shouted. "As soon as we're all set, we'll get Doc and Megan organised."

Jon's blood ran cold. While his body momentarily froze, his mind raced at a hundred miles an hour with one thought uppermost.

His Megan could be killed if they carried out such a risky plan and something went wrong.

Megan!

Dead!

How could he live without her? Nausea roiled in his gut as the full import of his fears burst upon him, driving him to protest vociferously.

"She can't do that! It's too dangerous. What if things go wrong? Megan could be hurt. Killed maybe. There's jagged metal sticking out everywhere. The car could roll, with Megan in it. If it ends up in the river, she could be drowned."

He shuddered, visualising the myriad images of death and destruction reeling across his horrified imagination.

How could they consider for even one moment, letting Megan put herself in such danger? He couldn't be a party to it. He just couldn't. Megan's life was too precious to risk.

It was Megan herself who answered him, fear causing her to shout angrily at him.

"You're right Jon. I might get hurt, or killed, if anything goes wrong. So it's up to you, I reckon. If you do your job right, I'll be safe. Come on, snap out of it! A man's dying down there and you're wasting time."

Without waiting for an answer, she plunged down the bank in the doctor's wake, intent on helping to the best of her ability.

Grimly admitting defeat, Jon got on with it, rapidly double checking every connection. Megan was trusting him with her life. He wouldn't, couldn't, let her down.

He couldn't afford to, because without Megan, his life would be worthless. A vitally important revelation had just now flashed into his brain. He thrust it aside to study later, when this emergency was over. Right now he was too busy making sure the danger to his woman was minimised as far as possible.

Revelation would have to wait its turn.

Stabilising both the patient and his car was achieved in record time. With Jonathon and Don lifting and supporting her on the steep slope, Megan climbed up and wriggled awkwardly, feet first, through the window, scraping her arm on the broken frame as she did so. Sparing a quick glance, she saw she was bleeding sluggishly from a long, shallow gash.

Painful. Not serious.

Megan ignored it, concentrating on following Doc's orders.

The man had lapsed into unconsciousness and Doc was urging her to check the state of his legs while he rigged the IV. Crouching in the confined space, she confirmed Doc's worst fears.

Blood was pooling on the floor from lacerations to his left leg, the one that was crushed and broken. Acting quickly, Megan applied a tourniquet as directed to stem the bleeding, then braced herself to support the injured man while the men separated the two wrecks.

As the squeal of tortured metal pierced her eardrums, Megan prayed the liberal application of fire retardant foam would prevent any sparks from igniting the spilt petrol she could smell.

Megan was scared. Really scared.

It was true she'd helped at accident scenes before. Because of that, she'd taken first aid lessons and regular refresher courses to keep her skills up to date.

What she had never done, however, was put herself in direct danger. She knew exactly how perilous her position was, and the knowledge terrified her.

The small vehicle rocked against its hastily placed supports. Tearing metal screamed as it was slowly freed from the weight of the station wagon pressing down on it.

Megan prayed aloud. A litany of formless pleas for deliverance, never once releasing her grip on the IV bag she held up with her right hand, or the tourniquet held by her left hand. Using her body weight to hold him steady, she leaned into the injured man.

A final jerk, and separation was achieved.

The little car rocked violently, slipping away from the gum tree that had halted its initial plunge towards the river. Feeling the movement at the same time she heard Don's shout of alarm, Megan braced herself, her mind going blank until she felt the jolt as the two cables took the weight. And held it.

Hardly daring to breathe, Megan opened eyes she hadn't realised were closed, and glanced around her. The car had slewed right round.

She was looking straight down at the water through the broken windscreen, her unconscious patient leaning forward heavily against his seatbelt.

Don, calling reassuringly that they'd soon have her out safely, began to prise open the warped driver's door.

Gasping with relief, Megan answered the doctor's questions, carrying out the checks he asked for, unaware of the tears streaming down her face.

Staying where she was, she gave Doc, leaning in through the now open door, what assistance she could, while the station wagon was winched up to the road where it could no longer threaten to roll back down on them. Wailing sirens signalled the arrival of the ambulance with its crew of paramedics.

In no time at all, it seemed, the injured man had been carefully extricated and strapped to a stretcher, with Doc Rogers preparing him for the dash to hospital. The other driver, shocked and badly shaken up, was sent with them.

Tenderly, Jon helped Megan climb out of the wreckage. Her knees buckled, too weak to support her. She collapsed to the ground, head between her knees, breath rasping in her throat, as she struggled against the sudden weakness.

Jon's arms stayed around her, supporting her; his voice murmuring words she was too dazed to interpret, although she drew strength from their gentle, loving tone.

The doubts she'd been struggling with dissipated as she leaned against him, feeling the strong beat of his heart under her cheek.

No way was she going to refuse this man.

She loved him too much to let doubt stand in the way of her chance at happiness. If he didn't love her already, she'd teach him to.

Lights flashing, the ambulance left and Doc Rogers rejoined them, congratulating Megan.

Still shaky, she scrambled to her feet, and with Jon on one side and the burly policeman on the other, clambered back up to the road.

"Being a heroine is pretty tough going, eh Meggie," Doc sympathised. "Here, let me have a look at that arm. Any other cuts or scrapes? No? I think you should come back with me. I'll get you cleaned up and give you something to help you sleep. Come along girl, these two can finish up here without us."

Longing to protest; to stay at Jon's side, Megan allowed herself to be led away.

Jon still had a job to do and she was exhausted. The whole episode had taken only a few minutes, but its intensity had sapped her strength. Turning as she stepped into the doctor's car, Megan flashed Jon a tired, sweet smile. A smile which was answered by one of equal sweetness.

Long after midnight, Jon finally parked the tow-truck in the garage. He had made two trips, bringing in the wrecks, and helped Don clear the broken glass and oil spills off the road. His part in the proceedings was over. Accident investigators would take over now.

Megan's house was in darkness. She'd be asleep, especially if she'd swallowed Doc's sleeping pill. Jon didn't expect her to wake till late.

Besides, he had some serious thinking to do before he spoke to Megan again.

Sleep first, though. He was too tired to think straight at that moment.

In a sober, pensive mood, Jon cut a bouquet of Megan's favourite roses, a very small bouquet after the previous day's depredations, and headed for her door in the middle of the morning. Knocking and walking straight in as had become his custom lately, he was disconcerted to find Megan was not alone. Of course she wasn't. News of her exploit was all over town, and friends agog with curiosity wanted to hear the full story from the lips of the heroine of the hour. Plunking the flowers in a mug on the kitchen sink, he joined them in the lounge room.

"Feeling better this morning, Meggie? How about the arm?" Self-consciousness reduced him to banal platitudes, when he was bursting to utter memorable words. Privately. Assured Megan was fine, he tossed a quick, 'See you later' over his shoulder, and departed.

It was nice to have friends, yet Megan wished she'd been alone when Jon came in. He'd looked very subdued, as if he had something heavy on his mind.

Pleading tiredness, not a lie at all, she finally closed the door on her visitors. Jon had said he'd see her later, so she curled up on the sofa to wait for him, dozing off immediately.

~~~~~

Time to wheel out the Harley, Jon decided. Megan enjoyed riding on the Harley, and he wanted her undivided attention. Dingo Hill would be far enough out of town.

He got the bike ready, and waited for her visitors to leave.

Keeping a surreptitious eye on her door, he bided his time, playing half-heartedly with Trixie.

~~~~~

Opening her eyes after her nap, Megan was startled to discover Jon sitting opposite, watching her intently. Seeing she was awake, he smiled, inviting her to go for a ride with him.

"It'll do you good, Meggie. A bit of fresh air and sunshine." He held his hand out to her, helping her up from the sofa.

Megan didn't need asking twice. She'd persuade him to stop, somewhere far away from well-meaning interruptions, and bring the conversation round to his unanswered proposal. Hastily pulling on boots and jacket, she reached for the helmet Jon held out to her. The glint of something bright caught her eye. Looking closely, Megan picked out the single strand of long, red hair snagged in the lining, holding it up to the light.

"Someone's been wearing my helmet, and left her hair behind," she uttered in a Papa Bear growl.

Jon chuckled. Megan had woken in a cheerful mood. Fearing rejection following his monumental gaffe the previous night, he'd expected to have a hard time persuading her to accompany him. If she was capable of joking, maybe all his bridges hadn't been burnt after all.

"Angie of course." Jon stated the obvious. There was only one source of hair that colour in Oxley Crossing.

"Would you believe it, Megan, she came banging on the door yesterday morning, waking me up at some ungodly hour to take her out to 'Morgan's Run'."

Jon shook his head at Angie Wilson's antics.

"Said she had to see Alan before he left for Tamworth. Since she doesn't have a car, she thought I wouldn't mind being hauled out of bed to take her." He grinned, inviting Megan to share his amusement.

"She really did that?" Megan blinked owlishly. "Came and woke you up to drive her out there? Why didn't she just phone him?"

Now she knew what had happened yesterday, and what a relief it was to be proved guilty of jumping to false conclusions. She vaguely recalled hearing Jon ride out while she wallowed in misery.

"Phoning seemed logical to me, too, but apparently they'd had another of their rows and she was afraid he might hang up on her. I didn't wait around to get involved; just let her off outside the house and rode straight back to town."

Laughing with Jon, Megan felt light-hearted now that that little mystery was solved; and solved so satisfactorily. She put her helmet on and swung up behind Jon, eager to be off before anyone could prevent their departure.

Neither of them noticed the knowing smiles that followed their progress down Bridge Street and across the creek. Megan Patterson on the back of Jon Armitage's Harley was becoming a very familiar sight in Oxley Crossing.

~~~~~

Sitting on top of Dingo Hill, Megan companionably at his side, Jon marshalled his thoughts.

When he felt ready, he turned to face Megan, holding her lightly by both shoulders, eyes locked earnestly on hers.

"Megan, you asked me last night why I wanted to marry you, and I gave you a long list of reasons, all quite true. At that time, I believed them to be the whole truth. I didn't know it then, but they weren't. Not the whole truth."

Megan's eyes clung to his apprehensively. Surely he wasn't withdrawing his proposal! Not when she'd made up her mind to accept.

"Also, I said I was glad I wasn't in love. Now I know that wasn't true at all. I didn't know what love is when I said that. Now I do, Meggie."

Jon took a deep breath. The next bit was the hardest. Would Megan believe him, or would she think he was making it up, lying to win back the ground he'd lost last night?

Jon prayed for divine guidance.

"Last night, when I was terrified for your safety, it hit me like a giant fist into my stomach. I knew, without any doubts whatsoever, why you've become so important to me. All the barriers I've erected round my heart came crashing down, leaving my emotions stripped bare, and I knew. I just *knew.* I love you."

This was harder than he thought, but Megan needed to hear the words, so he drew a deep breath and continued.

"It's nothing like the airy-fairy emotion I used to believe love was. What I feel for you, Meggie, is an absolute truth. Wild and exciting; gut-wrenching in its intensity, yet gentle and incredibly warm and comforting at the same time."

Anxious, Jon paused, hoping his words were sufficient for his cause. He wasn't entirely comfortable trying to explain his emotions. Megan's glowing countenance encouraged him to go on.

"I'm asking again Megan. Not because you're my friend, or would be a good mother for my children or any of those other reasons I gave you, but because I love you. With my whole heart, body and soul. I love you Megan. Now and forever."

The words flowed from his lips, more easily each time he said them.

"Megan Patterson, will you marry me?"

Joyfully, Megan flung her arms around Jon's neck, kissing him wildly, happy beyond all expectations.

Jon loved her.

Loved her as she'd always yearned to be loved. Tears streamed down her cheeks, although as she drew back, she laughed at the same time for the sheer joy of being alive and in love.

Wiping her tears away with his fingers, Jon studied them in wonder.

"Happy tears. They are *happy* tears, aren't they Meggie?"

Megan nodded, her radiant smile chasing away past storms. Jon laughed with her, and kissed her back with all the pent-up longing contained within him. Leaning back to catch his breath, he gazed into Megan's starry eyes.

"Do I take it you're accepting me then?" His voice was husky with emotion.

"Oh yes, Jon! Yes! Yes! Yes! I love you too, you know. I've loved you for ages. Probably from the first time I saw you, when I felt a tingling little surge of electricity when our fingers accidentally touched."

"I felt it too. It scared the life out of me," Jon confessed sheepishly. "I must have subconsciously known I'd met my destiny."

"I've grown to like it. A lot." Shyness brought a blush to Megan's cheeks. She wasn't any more used to confiding her feelings than Jon was. "It makes me feel so special; all warm and alive in a way I've never felt with anyone else."

"I feel the same. It sure makes kissing you more exciting than kissing anyone else has ever been."

Jon proceeded to demonstrate, to Megan's complete satisfaction.

Later, much later, Jon fetched a tiny jeweller's box covered in worn blue velvet from his saddlebags.

"These were my mother's wedding and engagement rings," he explained, showing the contents to Megan. "She left them to me, with instructions to give them to the woman I loved. Dad got them out of his safety deposit box after meeting you, and sent them to me. Said he thought I might be needing them."

Jon grinned, then sobered, looking doubtfully at Megan. "Do you like them Meggie?"

"They're beautiful, Jon; and being your mother's makes them extra special."

Lifting the lovely ring set with two heart shaped diamonds out of the box, Jon slid it onto Megan's finger. A perfect fit.

A good omen for their future together.

Jon kissed the finger bearing his ring, then Megan's lips.

"Don't make me wait too long, will you Meggie? Now I finally know my heart's true desire, I can't bear to wait a moment longer than necessary."

A short engagement suited Megan too.

Edith and Mike were due back in a few days. She would enlist her new step-mother's assistance in organising their wedding. The intimate family celebration they both preferred wouldn't take a lot of time to arrange.

Only Edith's personal satisfaction over her step-daughter's engagement compensated her for missing out on all the drama. Charged with helping Megan organise her wedding, Edith threw herself into the task whole-heartedly.

Which was why, when a radiantly happy Megan, wearing her mother's elegant Edwardian styled wedding gown, walked down the aisle on her father's arm, it was in front of a considerably larger congregation than the intimate family gathering she'd envisaged.

Not that Megan noticed the overflowing pews. Her eyes were fixed on just one figure; the handsome groom, whose eyes were riveted unwaveringly upon her, his love for her shining proudly for all to see. Their eyes meeting, they shared a special, very private smile as she joined him, confidently placing her hand in his.

Geni Sullivan and Megan's cousin Margaret had done sterling duty as bridesmaids. Jon, of course, had his brother Gordon for best man.

In the best of wedding traditions, Jon's father had tears of joy glistening in his eyes as he'd kissed his brand-new daughter-in-law. Tears amply matched by those of Megan's own father; Edith's being tempered by pride in her achievement. To listen to her, one would imagine it was all due to her machinations that the two young lovers had overcome the obstacles in their path to true happiness.

It was a wedding to remember; all the matrons of Oxley Crossing agreed. What a pity Jenny Patterson hadn't lived to see her daughter walk down the aisle. Well, all the excitement was over now.

Until the next wedding, of course. They hadn't missed the way young Sophie James blushed and turned to look at Bob Whitman when she caught Megan's bouquet.

~~~~~

Running down the stairs after changing out of her wedding dress, Megan surprised them all yet again. Her going away outfit was most definitely non-traditional. She wore Jon's special bridal gift – her own set of leathers, black to match his own.

Amidst a shower of confetti the two roared off into the night; to discover heaven on earth in each other's arms at their secret honeymoon destination.

THE END

I hope that you enjoyed 'Saving Jonathon Armitage'.

Turn the page for a preview of the next book in the 'Love in Oxley Crossing' Series – 'Finding Mr Wright'.

Here is Your Preview of
Finding Mr Wright

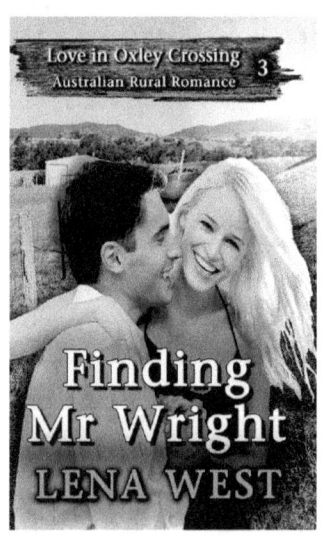

1

"Megan! Guess what! I've found Mr Right!"

Her mind still lost in the column of numbers, Megan Armitage marked her place with her finger and looked up.

"What?"

Geni Sullivan, her friend and also her business partner as from today, laughed, a blush staining her cheeks beneath her carefully applied make-up

"You know how I'm always raving on about there being one perfect man, our Mr Right, for each of us? Like your Jon for you?"

Megan nodded, wondering what nonsense Geni was on about now. Her friend was noted for exaggeration and hyperbole where men were concerned.

Although…. Megan frowned. Geni had been acting strangely ever since her arrival in Oxley Crossing the week before. Quiet and subdued. Not at all her usual exuberant self, and, until now, no mention of her accustomed favourite topic of conversation – men. Even now there appeared to be an almost hysterical tinge to her excitement. To tell the truth, Megan was rather concerned about Geni, without any idea of exactly why she should be, so she paid closer attention to the conversation than she normally would have.

"Well. This morning when I enrolled Jamie in school, we were waiting in the corridor when the door next to us opened and out stepped that gorgeous hunk I met at your wedding last year. You know, tall, brown eyes, dark hair silvering at the temples. Looks like he works out regularly."

A grin flitted across Megan's face as she recognised the man Geni described, but she didn't interrupt the flow. This was more like the Geni she knew and loved. Maybe she had simply been feeling stressed over the move and settling into a new town. Country life was way different to what her friend was used to in Sydney.

"He stepped up to me, hand out, and said, 'I remember you. We met at Megan's and Jon's wedding. Jenny, isn't it? I'm Ben Wright, the school principal.' My heart was fluttering so madly I barely heard him, but I grabbed his hand, and like an idiot said, 'Geni Sullivan. Accountant and mother of Jamie.'"

Geni laughed again, fanning her hand in front of her face. "I tell you Megan, that man is hot!"

This time it was Megan's turn to laugh, partly with relief that her friend was back to what constituted normal for her, and partly at the new image of the school principal which Geni had planted in her mind. Sure, Ben was good-looking in a quiet, studious way, and several local women had made unsuccessful plays for him, but she would never have thought to describe him as 'hot'.

Interestingly, the faint blush staining Geni's cheeks fluctuated as she continued. "It wasn't until he shook Jamie's hand as well and I heard the kid say, 'Nice to meet you, Mr Wright,' that the name registered. At the wedding we were just Ben and Geni. When we came here to live I hoped … wondered, I mean, if I'd meet him again. But still, it took me by surprise this morning to run into him when I least expected it."

Genie wandered into the kitchenette next separating their offices and put the kettle on.

"Just think Megan," she called over her shoulder. "His name. He's Mr Wright. Spelt with a 'W'. I checked the spelling on his nametag, but what a coincidence, eh. Reckon the butterflies in my tum mean he could be 'The One'? My Mr Right?"

Megan shook her head as she made her own way to the coffee machine.

Geni was unbelievable, but she was her best friend. Had been since the day they'd found themselves assigned to adjoining desks in the Australian Taxation Office in Sydney, and she was so happy to see her acting like herself again.

Although Geni was several years older than herself, they had hit it off immediately; the biggest difference between them being Geni's perpetual search for her 'Mr Right'.

What a turn-up for the books if that elusive gentleman really did prove to be sober, serious Ben Wright.

"You never know, Geni. And love is in the air, or maybe the water, here in The Crossing. First Dad and Eddie, then Jon and I, Angie and Alan, and just lately I've been hearing whispers on the bush telegraph about Sophie James and Bob Whitman. So who knows; maybe you and Ben will be next."

The smile left her face, and all at once she was frowning slightly. "A word of warning, though, Geni. Ben was married, and by all accounts was deeply in love with his wife. She died. Leukemia I think. Anyway, it was very tragic, and he was still grieving when he arrived in The Crossing. Be kind to him Geni. Think carefully about his feelings before you get involved with him."

"Oh, you needn't worry. I won't be getting involved with anyone. I'm through with men for the foreseeable future. It was just that I was struck by the coincidence of his name."

Suddenly, before Megan's eyes, it was as if a light had been switched off, leaving her lively, vivacious friend looking lost, and, almost impossible to believe, afraid. Afraid, and almost hopeless. Worry flooded Megan again, worse than previously. This was so not Geni. Whatever did Geni have to be afraid of? Something was seriously wrong with her friend.

A client's arrival for his appointment meant she had to set the issue aside for now, but she made a mental note to get to the bottom of the mystery ASAP.

〰〰〰〰〰

Ben couldn't get back to the safety of his office fast enough.

That woman, with her sleek, platinum hair and green eyes had invaded his mind far too often for comfort since he'd danced with her at the wedding. When he'd heard Megan, the town's sole accountant, was taking on a partner who was an old friend from her Sydney days, he'd wondered if it could be the same woman who haunted his dreams.

Coming straight from a meeting with his senior staff members, his mind occupied by classroom logistics, to find himself face to face with her, had momentarily floored him. Only his well-honed social skills had saved him from making a complete ass of himself in front of the dozen or so curious staff, parents and kids milling around in the foyer.

Even more embarrassing had been getting her name wrong; but when they met at the wedding he'd been so dazzled he hadn't been capable of taking in such irrelevancies as names.

God, I was almost drooling over the woman! He continued to beat himself up. *Then she went and introduced her son!*

He could still hear her voice chirping brightly, warning him off, when she stated, '... mother of Jamie.' Mother! *Was that a discreet way of telling me she's married?*

While every fibre of his being urged him to make a play for her, his practical common sense dictated the exact opposite. His sexual awareness of her made him vulnerable; a feeling he didn't like.

There was no way he'd lay himself open to losing the respect of his friends and neighbours in Oxley Crossing by chasing after a married woman. A married woman who was the mother of one of his students.

~~~~~

Jamie Sullivan perched on the corner of his mother's desk, legs swinging as he recounted the highlights of his first day at Oxley Crossing Central School in between inhaling chocolate chip cookies and juice.

"... and my teacher is Mrs Johnson. She's old, but she seems pretty cool. Jack says we're lucky we got her and not Mr Reilly. Jack says he's a real nark. He sends more kids to detention than any other teacher in the whole school. It feels really odd, you know, Mum. Having high school kids at the same school as us younger ones. We've been teamed up with a year nine class for Peer Support, Mrs Johnson says. I wonder if that means we have to go across to the High School buildings or if they'll come to us?"

His tongue slowed long enough for him to take a much needed breath, cram another cookie into his mouth, and for his mother to slip a question in edgeways.

"What about that Mr Wright we met this morning? Will you be seeing anything of him?"

"Hardly, Mum. Mr Wright's the principal of the whole school. Mrs Cummings is in charge of our part. But Jack says Mr Wright coaches the Under Eleven soccer team this year. That's Jack's team, and he said I can join if I want. Can I, Mum?"

"I don't see why not. I'll find out about it tomorrow."

"No need. Jack says he'll take me to training on Wednesday evening across on the Oval. Can I go and play footie in the park now? Jack and the others will be waiting for me."

Receiving an affirmative from his mother, he scoffed a last cookie and ran off to join his new mates, leaving Genie gazing fondly after him, glad to know he'd found his feet so quickly, although she had a suspicion she was going to get tired very of hearing the words, 'Jack says.'. All the same, she intended to keep an especially close eye on him until she knew for sure they were safe here in Oxley Crossing.

There was no way she would let anyone, anyone at all, harm her son.

Continued…….

About the Author

Born in tropical North Queensland, Lena loves living close to the sea, although she moved frequently during her early years, living everywhere from large cities to isolated farms. Her most recent home has a deck overlooking the ocean, which is her favourite room in the house, for reading, writing, art, craft or even birdwatching, when the local birds come to visit.

After working as a primary school teacher in both her native Queensland, and later in New South Wales where she met her own romantic hero, she took a very early retirement to travel Australia with him, in a motorhome. This idyllic lifestyle lasted several years, during which time she indulged in the creation of story plots and their settings, culminating in her taking steps to fulfil her lifelong ambition to write.

Storytelling came naturally - she had been making up stories for her own entertainment all her life, but it wasn't until she began traveling that she had time to write down some of her favourites. Now published, *Marrying Alan Morgan*, is the first in a series of rural romances set in the fictional town of Oxley Crossing. It is followed by the soon to be released second in the series, *Saving Jonathon Armitage,* with several more in the series planned. She also writes standalone contemporary romances and Australian historical romances.

She has an addiction to happily-ever-afters, in both her reading and her own stories, so the romance genre was a natural fit, and the variety of places she has lived have all added to the settings in which she brings love to life.

You can find Lena on Facebook at:

https://www.facebook.com/LenaWestAuthor/

or sign up for her newsletter at :

www.lenawestauthor.com

Other Books by Lena West

Standalone Contemporary Romances

Loving Fenella (Coming 2018)

Bronwyn's Family (Coming soon)

Contemporary Series

The Wylde Flower Series (Coming soon)

Historical romances

Unto Death (Coming 2018)

Emily's Baby (Coming soon)

Home is the Heart (Coming soon)

Blue Streak (Coming soon)

Love and War (Coming soon)

Books in the
Love in Oxley Crossing Series

Marrying Alan Morgan

Saving Jonathon Armitage

Finding Mr Wright (Coming 2018)

Electing Robert Whitman (Coming soon)

Redeeming Josh Marten (Coming soon)

Connect with Lena

Be the first to know about it when Lena's next book is released!

Sign up to Lena's newsletter at

www.lenawestauthor.com

www.ingramcontent.com/pod-product-compliance
Lightning Source LLC
Chambersburg PA
CBHW061921130726
47908CB00016B/728